SHEBAT LEGION

Cover Illustration: Blue Shebat by Klarissa Kocsis
Cover and Book Interior Design: **Dreams2media**
Introduction by Beth W. Patterson
Ebook ISBN 978-1-9995380-1-9
Print ISBN 978-1-9995380-0-2

DEDICATION

To my mother, Klarissa Kocsis, thank you for your words of inspiration and support through the years.
To my father, Marco Katic, thank you for your words of wisdom.
To my husband, James, thank you for your words of faith and devotion.
To my children, Adam and Emily, all the words ever written.

"Into the labyrinth
Cut down to just a tenth
Nothing to face but your thoughts
Omen and oracle
Phantasmagorical
Casting and drawing their lots"
–Beth Patterson, "Labyrinth"

When Shebat asked me to write the forward for her book and include a lyric of mine, this was what immediately popped into my head. Because who wouldn't want to enter the labyrinth of Shebat Legion? It's a domain that is at once innocent, terrifying, playful, and resilient. Step right up and see what's inside!

You might fall down an unexpected trapdoor of surrealism. Or perhaps you'll wander the hall of mirrors and catch a glimpse of your distorted reflection in the silly and erotic, the sensual and poignant. Who knows? It's her realm, and we are all damned lucky to have found it in the first place. Sometimes it makes as much sense as a sparkly pink unicorn licking ichor from its fangs—and if that seems odd to you right now, it won't by the end of this tome. You might be be blindsided with whimsy or heartbreak, but you will never be disappointed. Each story is as unique as a zebra or a bloodstain.

I know this because I'm not only a fan of Shebat's, I'm also proud to call her a friend. We found each other when our stories ended up in the some of the same anthologies, we later shared personal stories with each other (from the crisis of uprooting to the solace we both found in Rush records), and we even got out of the same hell together. Since then, I've often found myself citing her works in my head, for they are colorful reminders of valuable lessons. Life doesn't always work the way it is "supposed to" by standards of the vast majority, but there is still enough love to go around for every obscure creature. Her tales make me feel less alone in this world.

Some people march to the beat of a different drum. Shebat takes her hubris one step further and completely reinvents the instrument, compelling us to follow along with her cadences. They are the battle cries of a survivor, the twelve-tone calls of a siren, or the purring of something cute and immortal that one might make the grave mistake of underestimating. Somebody broke the mold when Ms. Legion was made, but she herself ground it up to make glitter. She describes herself to me as the love child of Neil Gaiman and Trent Reznor, but I'm more inclined to deem her a cross between Hans Christian Andersen and Salvador Dali with a whiff of a Bette Midler narrative. And that's only scratching the surface.

Oh, and one last thing: the characters in the book are very much alive, and they're reading you right back. They find you most entertaining. Sleep well, kids.

--Beth W. Patterson

Beth W. Patterson was a full-time musician for over two decades before diving into the world of writing, a process she describes as "fleeing the circus to join the zoo". She is the author of the books *Mongrels and Misfits, The Wild Harmonic*, and a contributing writer to twenty anthologies.

Patterson has performed in eighteen countries across the Americas, Europe, Oceania, and Asia. Her playing appears on over a hundred and sixty albums, soundtracks, videos, commercials, and voice-overs (including seven solo albums of her own). More than a hundred of her compositions and co-writes have been released. She studied ethnomusicology at University College, Cork in Ireland and holds a Bachelor's degree in Music Therapy from Loyola University New Orleans.

Beth has occasionally worn other hats as a body paint model, film extra, minor role actor, recording studio partner, record label owner, producer, and visual artist. She is a lover of exquisitely stupid movies and a shameless fangirl of the band Rush. You can find her at www.bethpattersonmusic.com

CONTENTS

IT ALL STARTS WITH A POEM...

Paraseth was a winged colt
Blew he high on an upwind
White as white.

Star's twinkly-froth and oh,
All colts frisky, to have wings
Upon their back.

Ligja was a tiger, hungry.
Orange velvet,
sharp claws, purr.

He ate a dog
and left the bones
Beneath the kitchen rug.

Two-headed Clavus
Could speak in tongues.
He spoke Chinese better
than plates imagine.

He spoke French and German.
What a guy, what a guy.
But he couldn't waltz or tango.

Richard couldn't speak at all.
Remus was a rooster.

Brice liked to sit with his door to the wall.
Brice liked to say, "I take chances."
I could write forever
If my hand didn't tire.
My pen loving the paper
as a man to a whore.

I can word-lash and phrase-slice,
a slit-wristed deceiver.
Tread not where the heli-jest
Weevil-bost grow.

Paraseth Was a Winged Colt
By Shebat Legion

SILICON OAR

"Can you open your eyes for me?"

The soft voice intruded and then there was light.

"Follow my finger. Left. Now, right."

"Good." The voice sounded satisfied, and that made me happy.

I tried to smile but failed.

"Slowly," the voice cautioned.

"Where …" I tried to speak.

"Shush now," the voice said. "Let's try blinking."

Blinking. Yes. I could do that.

I blinked. Once, and then again and I heard a cluck of approval. I blinked again and she, (she?) laughed.

"Slow down. It will come to you."

I nodded or tried to nod, but nothing happened.

"Don't try to move," she, (it is a she) said. "Let's not get ahead of ourselves."

"Okay," I wanted to say. "I will be okay."

"You will be okay," she said.

It is later, and I have a tail. I move it back and forth, and it makes a swishing sound as if moving through water except that I know that is not true. I am on a table. Or in one.

"That is a pretty tail." I know her now, her name is Ruth.

I swish it because yes, it is a pretty tail. It has blue and green iridescent scales that glitter beneath the light. I would like to feel it move and I want to tell Ruth, but I can't.

"You will," Ruth said absently, "don't you worry."

So, I didn't worry, not then but later, I did.

"Shush," Ruth soothes as I scream without sound,

making my mouth if I had one, wide and gaping. I don't scream forever despite Ruth. Or maybe, now, in spite of Ruth.

"Where am I?" I want to ask. "What has happened to me?"

I know that something has happened to me.

"Everything is different," Ruth explained, "but you will be okay. You need to trust me."

I did try, but now it is different. She isn't telling me something, and I can't tell her that I know. But I *do* know! I know it in my bones if I have bones. I may not *have* bones! Do I have bones?

"I know you are frightened; you need to let yourself drift and understand, no one is trying to hurt you. The pain is behind you."

What does she mean? Behind me? Was I somewhere before? A location, behind of where I was in front? In front of what? And, where am I now? Why didn't she tell me?

"We are helping you. I am helping you. Me. Ruth."

"Ruth," I try to say without a mouth to say it, "I will not drift."

"Move your pretty tail."

I swish it angrily, splashing water that was not there on to the light, making Ruth laugh.

"You are a naughty girl."

Am I a girl?

I don't like Ruth.

Later.

The light is dark now, but I know it is later. I hear a door open because I can hear things now.

"Sorcha?" It is a soft-sounding voice.

Sorcha? Is that my name or is she asking me something?

"I am Selena."

Hello, I want to say. Who are you and who am I?

"I will be your night friend," she says. Another she.

"I am sitting beside you, and I have a book. I am going to read you a story from the book."

I try to nod.

"I know you like stories."

I nod again and then, with surprise, realize that I have nodded. Something. I have moved something. Did I nod my tail? Maybe it was that. Maybe it moved, and I felt it move!

"Once upon a time there lived a princess."

A princess. I nod my tail.

"She lived in a castle that overlooked a sparkling, blue lake."

Yes, it is real. I can feel my tail.

"Good." Selina sounds happy, and I feel my tail again, slapping it around and smacking it up and down, over and over.

"Okay, stop now," Selina laughs, and I would laugh too if I knew how and I think she knows that.

"Now, do you want to hear some more about the princess or do you want to smack your tail around some more? Just a little bit more, mind," she added. "Don't want to overdo."

I want to smack my tail around, and my face widens where my mouth is, and I scream but I am laughing.

"That is lovely," Selina says, and it is. It is lovely, this sound of my tail slapping and I laugh and laugh.

But it is later, and I stop because my tail hurts and I am not laughing anymore. My mouth widens even further, and I scream. I know she can hear me.

"Do you want to hear more about the princess?"

If I want to hear more about her, I must stop screaming, so I do.

"The princess had a mother and a father who loved her very much. They loved her so much they wanted to keep her safe forever, and they warned her about the pretty lake."

Tell me about the lake. I swish my tail, nodding. *The lake.*

"Because, while the lake was the prettiest lake in all the kingdom, it was very deep. A little princess could sink beneath the water, and not be able to breath, and then she would die."

This is not a nice story. I don't like it. I don't like it at all.

"The princess loved her mother and father with all of her heart and swore she would never go into the lake."

But one day she did. The princess goes into the lake. The princess always goes into the lake.

"Yes," Selina says in a sad voice. "The princess always goes into the lake."

Does she hear me?

Do you hear me, Selina?

"Yes. I can hear you."

I slap my tail. Why can't I hear me?

"You will."

Am I in the lake?

"One day, the princess went into the lake."

Am I the lake?

"No. Listen. Sorcha went into the lake."

But she loved her mother and father. I widen my mouth. *She did!*

"She did. And they loved her forever."

Am I Sorcha?

I reach out with my tail and feel the sound of the box around me.

"You are Sorcha."

Did I go into the lake?

"You are Sorcha, and you are in the lake."

I am in the lake now? No. I am in a box.

"There is a lake in the box, and you are Sorcha."

Am I a princess?

"Yes. And you went into the lake."

Did I die?

"You did."

Am I dead?

"Not anymore, not ever again." Selina soothed but my mouth opened wide, and so did my eyes.

I have eyes now.

"Shush now, baby," Selina croons. "Safe forever. A little princess."

In a box!

"In a lake," Selina corrected.

I can't stop screaming.

Forever?

"Forever."

MITTEN'S POCKETS

ZACHERY PHILLIP MITTEN LOVED TO collect things but nothing pleased him as much as his vast assortment of pockets. It was, perhaps, an odd thing to collect, but there it was. Pockets.

Of course, there were pockets, and then there were *pockets*.

There were several categories: utilitarian, the type left behind from denim jeans, more of a pouch. Or, from that same garment, the badge type of pocket, a flat pocket, plain or designed. There was the deep pocket, often found on aprons and then there was, as Zachery liked to think of them, the hobby pocket. The hobby pocket was an atypically shaped pocket, most often found on cargo pants or shirts. These pockets were Zackery's favorite type of pocket.

Zackery's great aunt Cornelia, a rather strange woman, had started and helped abet the pocket hobby. She had quite the collection built up over the years and Aunt and nephew sent packages of pockets to each other, through the mail, regularly. After Cornelia's death, her last will and testimony specified that her nephew should receive not only the bulk of her collection but a rare selection of never before mentioned pockets.

After a bottle of a particularly fine Merlot, Zackery raised his glass in memory of his Aunt and holding a pair of scissors to the string of his inheritance, fairly trembled in anticipation. He carefully removed the attached envelope, no doubt a letter from his deceased pocket mentor and then taking a shaky breath, he slid the scissors beneath the binding twine.

Snip went the scissors and with a careful rip, out spilled a multitude of pockets of every category and a smaller parcel wrapped tightly with packing tape. "Oh …" Zackery breathed. He sat on the floor in his living room, his collection of porcelain dolls smiling down at him in benevolence. "Thank you, Aunty Cornelia," he said. And he began to sort, saving the letter and the smaller package for dessert.

The utilitarians were set aside to be ironed before being placed in their special box. The badge pockets, all nice and flat, he left stacked. The deep pockets had already been carefully folded and could be stacked as well. The hobby pockets left him squirming with excitement for these were the crème de la crème. Misshaped, angular, cell phone pockets, pencil pockets, all different from the other, some closed with buttons, others with Velcro, or snaps, all in pristine condition. He lay them reverently on the carpet in front of him.

The idea of actually using the hobby pockets *for* something occurred to Zackery and not for the first time. He picked up a rather large hobby pocket, possibly removed from an army surplus item of clothing. It was deeper than it was wide, a long sturdy rectangle of a pocket and Zackery's mind raced. Why didn't people grow their own pockets? He had wondered this before. Kangaroos had them, why not people? A pocket of this magnitude would have untold uses if affixed to say, one's leg. Backpack straps and man purses were bunchy and uncomfortable. An actual leg pouch, if one could grow it, would be handy. It was a shame that you couldn't just sew them on your leg as you could do on another piece of material.

Then again, maybe you could.

So intrigued with the thought of sporting pockets, Zackery had paid a visit to a piercing parlor that specialized in alternative needs. "Well, no," The young man behind the counter had said. "We can't put pockets on you but what we can do is to insert metal loops and you could, you know, clip the bastards on, like."

But this was not a satisfying solution by any means and a disappointed Zackery left the shop without either loops or pockets.

Pockets sorted, Zackery turned his attention to the letter and the small bound parcel. The letter stated;

> *My dearest nephew. I leave to you my most prized possession, a collection of unusual pockets. I will tell you as I was told, do not release the pockets from their Ziploc pouches. I can only warn you; you will do as you choose. But I strongly urge you to leave them as undisturbed as I have. Thank you for being my hobby companion. I wish you the greatest happiness.*
>
> *Aunt C.*

With brow slightly furrowed, Zackery snipped at the tape around the small parcel, revealing an assortment of approximately twenty pockets, individually packed into vacuum sealed plastic baggies. Picking up first one bag and then another, Zackery frowned. They were hobby pockets, yes, which in itself was pleasing, but there seemed nothing unusual about them. He picked up his late Aunt's note again, looking on the other side of it to see if there was any more information. He looked through the packing; there was nothing to be found. Why were the pockets unusual? Had they belonged to famous people? He sat back on his heels, looking at the sealed pockets spread in front of him and then picked up one of the baggies containing a long rectangle of a pocket, made from what looked to be khaki. On the pocket was a loop, possibly used to clip on a pen or some other type of tool.

Like a hammer.

He carefully opened the plastic seal and slid the pocket out of its sleeve and examined it, turning it over in his hand. It was just a pocket, that and nothing more. Except, he thought as he held the pocket to his thigh, except it would look so lovely if he could wear it.

"*Yesssss.*" The voice said.

"Yes," Zackery mumbled, holding the pocket to his thigh again.

It was a perfect fit.

It could have been made just for him.

In a daze, Zackery stood up and went to his bedside table where he kept his sewing kit. He licked the end of a piece of thread and prepared the needle then slid out of his pants. He kicked them aside as he walked back into the living room, walking heedlessly over the stacked pockets he had sorted.

He grabbed the almost empty bottle of wine and splashed some of it on to his leg and began to sew the pocket to the outside of his thigh. His stitches were meticulous and as deeply sewn into the leg as possible. He used a tissue to blot the blood at first, finally resorting to using some of the utilitarians to staunch the flow. It took many pieces of the thread, but finally, Zackery had the hobby pocket sewn to his leg. He walked to the hall mirror and admired himself from different angles. Perfect.

"Hammerrrrrr."

Zackery did indeed have a small hammer, and he almost skipped to his tool box to fetch it, inserting it into the pocket with such enthusiasm that he became aroused. "Oh!" Zackery exclaimed, feeling foolish. He took the small hammer out of the pocket and slid the claw over the loop. "There!" With the blood still trickling down his leg and manhood at proud mast, he beamed at his reflection. Perfect.

"Hungryyyyyy …"

There came a knock on the door. Zackery all but pranced to open it, flinging the door wide open to the surprised look of his landlady, whose name was Glenda. She took one look at Zackery's pantless state and began to flee down the hallway. "Oh no." Zackery grinned as he caught her by the hair with one hand, his other hand on her mouth. "No, no."

He dragged her back into his apartment and shoved her down onto his couch. He reached for the hammer and held it in front of her face, holding his finger to his lips. Glenda nodded.

"Hungryyyy ..." The voice said, and Glenda made a rush for the door. Zackery caught her easily, rather surprised at his agility. He had never been much for sports. *"Hungry!"* The voice insisted.

"Can you hear that?" Zackery asked Glenda who continued to struggle, leaping from the couch and launching herself head first into Zackery's groin, mouth open and biting wildly. Zackery screamed but struck with the hammer anyway, hitting his landlady again and again. But as if she were a bulldog, she would not unhinge her teeth which eventually met in the middle. And still, she bit, clawing at his legs, tearing off the pocket with her nails even as she spat his penis to the carpeted floor.

"Nooooo ..." The voice screamed as Zackery fell backward, landing on his buttocks and then rolling into a ball, wailing. *"Hungry!"*

Glenda grabbed the hammer out of Zackery's flailing hand and beat at the pocket. "Devil, back to hell you go!" She screeched. "You. Are. Not. On. The. Lease!"

She pounded until there was a silence in the apartment except for Zackery's moans. She kept a careful distance as she phoned 911, eyeing the pockets on the floor and the one that had been sewn to Zackery's leg. "Demonlings." She spat, "worse than roaches."

She shoved the plastic covered pockets together into a pile with her foot, keeping an eye on Zackery as she waited for the ambulance. Edging past him, she snatched a throw from the couch and covered the pockets even as the paramedics rushed into the apartment, placed Zackery onto a stretcher and his penis into an insulated cooler.

Glenda refused medical treatment, gave her statement to the police and later and alone, took a broom and dustbin and swept up all the pockets, plastic covered or not, and dumped them into the incinerator, heaving a sigh of relief as she did.

At the hospital, Zackery's penis was sewn back on, and the wounds on his leg tended. Zackery never spoke again and was eventually placed in the state ward for the insane. But as one nurse was to say to the other as they gave the new addition a look over, "you have to admit, all the other stuff aside, having a sewn on pocket like that would be handy."

LAMP-BASTED

BRUCE NODDED AT THE TABLE lamp, and the table lamp nodded back. "Hey," said Bruce, as he tossed his jacket over a chair. "So, no. I didn't tell those guys." The lamp drooped slightly. Bruce patted the lamp, " You kinda had to be there. Trust me; they wouldn't have listened."

Lamp's lightbulb flickered. Bruce shrugged. "Fine, I'll tell you why."

"It was Wednesday at the pub and the small tap room filled. The usual crowd was in attendance."

"I'm not saying its aliens," Stan says, and then, Cherry says, "You sound like that guy," and then she pulls at her thigh highs over a shapely leg.

Lamp snorted.

So, Stan's and many other pairs of eyes follow Cherry's movement because, you know."

Lamp flickered.

"The guy with the hair," says Dwight, nodding, eyes glued to that twenty-something flesh revealed by the long stocking."

Lamp stiffened.

"I'm just sayin'," Stan was sayin', Bruce continued. "It was this burst in the sky and this thing, this shiny thing, hovering."

Lamp chittered.

"Cherry?" She is decorative to be sure, but once she starts talking, you want to crawl under a bar stool and bury your head in the floor. Or as Bullet puts it, "man, she is sweet to look at it, and she ain't stupid, but she has a bad case of Yap o'litus."

Lamp looked at Bruce and Bruce looked back at

Lamp. "Seriously," Bruce said. "And then Andrew Stag says, "I saw an alien once.""

"So did I," chimed in Barrie One - there are two Barries. He sneaks a look a Cherry who is applying yet another coat of lip gloss, and he is all but gritting his teeth."

Lamp squeaked.

"Why? He doesn't think it's fair that Cherry, who has recently come of age, is the daughter of someone who is a friend of almost everyone in the pub. You have to treat her like a daughter and end up getting into trouble with the Missus anyway, because yes, Cherry is just that pretty."

Lamp gasped.

"Not as pretty at *you* are."

Lamp cooed.

"So there you have Barry One sipping at his ale with a pinch of resentment, glowering."

Lamp chittered, and Bruce grinned. "So anyway, Andrew Stag says, "Oh yeah?" He glares at Andrew Stag, who at the ripe age of twenty-five, is allowed to court the luscious Cherry without fear of censure."

"I did," Andrew says with enthusiasm. "Cherry and I were out in the field, you know, the one in the back of Stedman's and we were, you know,"

"Get on it with it, man," Barrie One grumps.

"So then, Cherry leans forward, all tender cleavage that you could not look at if you valued your marital contentment, "it was a bright light.""

"Yes!" Stan breaks in, nodding with excitement, "all glowy and hovering and that."

Lamp flickered on and off briefly, and Bruce paused in his narrative. "Yes, I'm getting to it. Keep your cord on."

The lamp looked at him.

"That was a joke."

Lamp shrugged.

"Okay, fine. Well, you see, the boys at the pub …"

Lamp flickered again.

"Right, and that girl Cherry, and no, other than the bartender there were no other women, well, they kept talking about that light, see?"

Lamp looked out the window pensively.

"So, I was just sitting by myself, the way I do and Cherry starts floating."

Lamp blinked in enquiry.

"Ya, she was floating."

Lamp gestured a "go on" gesture.

Cherry floated up from her bar stool, legs waving ever so gently, her short skirt hiked above her thighs, and no man's eyes were not glued to the sight."

Lamp glowed in annoyance.

"Don't get mad. Cherry is not my type. Not my type at all. I'm just sayin'"

Lamp blinked.

"I'm not defending them. So anyway, Stan says, "There she goes again." And Cherry is sayin',

"They asked us all sorts of questions, and I had to take off my clothes and so did Steve."

"Andrew," Andrew corrected her.

"I meant Andrew, of course," Cherry giggles, floating.

"And we were searched, and they didn't find anything but they took samples and this one little gray guy, he must have been, he was, oh," she gushed, " soooooh cute!"

"And she does this huffy thing with her voice, like."

Lamp all but hopped off of the table with irritation.

"It doesn't matter to me what her voice sounds like, just sayin' she has an effect, like, on the guys at the pub. So anyway, she is going on like,

"And he had little tufts of hair on his little nose, and you could see he was trying to grow a mustache, and then he."

"And so on. The boys in the pub, me included, I won't lie, kept looking because you just can't help look when someone floats, but I admit, none of us were listening anymore if you know what I'm sayin'."

Lamp nodded impatiently.

"I'm getting to it. So then, Barry Two walks in."

Lamp clicked.

"Barrie's clone."

"Hi, Barry." He says, "Cherry floating again?" and Barry One nods to his clone and they both laugh. And Cherry is still talking away about who knows what and that is when Pricilla walked in."

Lamp tilted its head to the side.

"Pricilla is Stan's wife, and she sees Cherry floating and starts yelling at Stan."

Lamp glowed impatiently.

"Well, Stan's lustful thoughts were pretty loud, so I'm guessing she heard and that is why she came over to the pub. She doesn't usually."

Lamp sighed.

"The Barries tried to stop the fight, but once Pricilla begins the transformation, that bite of hers hurts something awful, and she is all, gnawing away on Cherry's leg. Cherry is screaming and then Ed, the pub owner came out like some high falutin' wizard and started tossing out telepathic dampers as if that was going to accomplish anything, which of course it didn't."

Lamp dimmed and then dimmed some more.

"Eventually, the bartender, and swear, I can never remember her name. She is a sprite, and they are secretive about stuff like that. Well, she grabs a club and starts hitting Pricilla with it until she lets go of Cherry who is sobbing over her missing leg and screaming about how she was going to sue for damages."

Lamp flashed on and off with emphasis.

"Well, sure she could just grow a new one, but why should she? It wasn't like she was asking for it and, the truth is, I did think Pricilla went overboard. A man can't always help what he is thinking, and Stan was trying not to think it, you know?"

Lamp dimmed dismally, then flashed with anger and chittering away, lectured sternly.

Bruce nodded and nodded again, trying to get in a word edgewise but Lamp would have none of it.

"!"

"Yes. You are right, she."

"!!? !!!"

"I know, but."

"!!!!"

"He isn't that bad a guy, he."

"????"

Bruce tried to hug Lamp but was shrugged away. Bruce looked at Lamp and said, "And that was when the local gang of bloodsuckers walked in and started playing Euchre, and old Lucas gets up from his corner where he sits all moldy and rotted, and he starts playing guitar. That always starts a good jam, and before you know it, it's two a.m. Cherry is drunk, and Andrew is helping her hop out of the pub, and people are leaving except for Lucas who starts crawling back underneath the pub floor where he lives. So I come home, and that's why I didn't tell anyone about you."

Lamp turned it's back, but then looked over its shoulder, raising its shade slightly.

"Just because it was busy, doesn't mean I don't want them to meet you."

Lamp gave the tiniest of flickers.

"Sure you can come to the pub. It's better that way, anyhow, like."

Bruce patted the lamp and then slid out of his body, slithering with it to the closet where he hung it up carefully. The lamp watched mournfully from its corner by the window.

"We can go tomorrow if you want."

Lamp squirmed.

"Sure they will like you," Bruce bubbled. "They are going to love you."

WHATEVER LOLA WANTS

Summary: A poet takes refuge in her sister's house, but is greeted by her nemesis.

ON A COLD DAY, ANNIE the poet walks toward her sister's house.

Annie took out a key and jammed it into the lock with, as always, a poem on her lips and rage in her heart. "She stomped in anger to her sister's door. It was a last resort and nothing more. She snarled at the lock that would not budge to her key. 'The front lock is tricky and stubborn, like me.'"

Annie nodded with satisfaction, her words puffs of icy smoke in the frigid air. "The key would not turn, and she yet again swore, as a sudden shrill yelp came from behind the locked door." Annie grimaced. It was her sister's dog. She tried the door again, muttering.

"Suzette's husband had died, and he had been rich. They'd had no kids, and Suzette was his bitch." Annie snickered. "She shivered and pushed as did the wind's blast, but the key won the battle, the knob turned at last."

Annie grinned, but it faded quickly. She frowned and retreated to familiar ground. "The wind tossed her sideways and into the hall, where over her sister's dog Annie did fall."

But there came a low . . . call?

Startled, Annie shook both her head and the fledgling poem away. There was a snarling bark and Annie stared at the beast. Her sister's dog was small, true, but perhaps harmless was not the best way to describe it.

And it was quite strange looking; with gray tufts of hair and long, prehensile toes. It looked more like an oversized rat than a dog. It growled again, staring her down with bright, button-like eyes.

"Lola! Bad girl!" Annie scolded and continued with her poem. "As if the thing had been coughed up from Hell, the little dog lifted a lip to drown out her yell. With its one ear askew, its thin tail brushed the tile. 'Shoo', Annie said, 'you are incredibly vile.'"

Annie kicked at the dog as she walked into her sister's house.

From its mouth—raised to the heavens, all beseeching—came a sound as if demons from Hell began screeching.

The words again came unbidden. Annie froze and stared at the small dog. "What?"

The dog screeched again. Annie clutched at the wall. She gave a small shudder and then ran down the hall.

"Suzette?"

The words hung in the hall like a wet cloak.

Annie gave the dog a sideways look and edged down the corridor to where she assumed the kitchen waited.

The dog seemed to smile, its teeth unnaturally white. Annie pushed it away as she shivered in fright.

"Who keeps talking? Suzette? Are you here?" Annie called, and the dog cocked an ear.

Now Annie was not of the dog-loving breed, but jobs had been scarce and her coin gone to greed. She cursed Lola sternly and rose to her knees, "You are such a bad dog!" The dog gave a sneeze.

When Lola sneezed, Annie fumbled in panic at the wall and the light switch. The dog rushed at her, and she backed into the door. "Suzette? This isn't funny, where are you?"

The little dog barked and then seemed to sneer. "Who do you think you are, coming in here?"

Annie pushed open a door at the end of the hall. The kitchen was large, facing the back yard, covered almost entirely in garish, dog-themed wallpaper, but no Suzette.

The dog ran to its bowl on the linoleum floor, and, like Poe's Raven, Annie yelled out, "Nevermore!"

"Be quiet!" Annie hissed. She rubbed her sore eyes. Oh, she was so tired, and more, she was tired of being tired. Her mind sometimes played tricks on her and was in full playmate mode today, it seemed.

Lola sat down on the floor, facing her, tail waving tentatively.

"Go back to Hell," Annie whispered, and the dog seemed to say, "I have a right to this house! You go away!"

"Dogs don't talk," she informed Lola, who then crouched in a curious fashion.

Annie stared and then frowned. Lola began to jump like a deer, up and down.

"My god, what the hell are you doing?"

Lola, with lips pulled back into a leer, raised her hackles and growled, "You are not wanted here!"

Lola continued jumping. Her small feet barely touched the ground before she launched into the air again. Annie eyed Lola warily.

In a panic, Annie ran toward carpeted steps, from the dining room up to where bedrooms were kept.

Annie placed a hand on either side of her head and walked carefully toward the staircase. The little dog stopped jumping, gave a series of yaps, and then followed close on her heels. "Be quiet. Enough poetry for one day," Annie said.

The dog stopped, stared, and cocked its small head; its hostile expression filling Annie with dread.

"Knock it off," Annie reprimanded Lola. And then she said to the poem or the dog in its stead, "If you don't shut up you will never get fed."

The dog became silent, it's small tail just a' wagging. Annie gave a victorious, "Ha! I won!"

"Now you're just bragging," the voice taunted.

Annie looked around wildly and shook her head. "Man, I *must* be tired. Suzette?" she called again. "Is that you? Stop trying to scare me. Where are you?"

The late afternoon sun cast its deep winter shade; the wind howled with laughter at the expression she made.

"Suzette?"

A tiny four-poster bed graced a rag-braided mat. Lace crocheted slippers were placed beside that. On the walls hung paintings that all seemed to say, "What are you doing here? Please go away!"

"My God!" Annie gasped and clutched at the bedstead. "Enough with the poetry, try talking instead! I mean, just talk. No more rhymes! No more rhymes!"

She looked around the dog's room as she rubbed at her head. There was a pink satin-covered crib that matched the small bed.

"Enough with the damned poetry," Annie quietly said.

Still the dog followed her, howling instead.

"Suzette!" Annie shrieked. "Stop playing games. I can play, too."

But this is so fun and I'm better than you!

"What is going on?"

There came a screech like a nail scraping a plate; a wail of a promise, of shadows and hate.

Annie backed up 'til the backs of her knees touched the bed. "That dog," she whispered. "It must want me dead."

They say dogs can smell fear and, Annie supposed, the dog would catch the scent despite its small nose.

"Stop it, stop it!" Annie wailed, covering her ears. "Suzette!"

"It's only a dog," Annie said sadly, then noticed a pie and reached for it gladly.

"What pie?" Annie screamed. "What pie? There is no bloody pie!"

It's cherry, my favorite, she thought as she ate it. Which was perhaps her last thought as she choked on the pit. The dog lay against her and started to gloat. Annie sprawled on the floor and continued to choke.

Lola lifted her lip in a satisfied grin, and that is when Annie's sister finally walked in.

Suzette rushed to her sister's aid, but she was too late. The cherry pit in her throat had sealed Annie's fate.

Or perhaps more than Fate had put on a good show? Lola can't tell us, so we'll never know.

FATHER'S DAY

"This cannot be good for your soul." Jason whispered aghast, as he viewed the remains of whatever was left chopped up and bloody, on Ashley's kitchen counter.

Ashely ignored it and the comment and poured a cup of coffee which he refused.

"Ashely ..." His voice trailed off as she looked at him, a stony expression on her pretty face, a face that appeared innocent until you stared into her eyes.

Jason cleared his throat nervously. "Ashley. Look. I think it is cool that you are into all that magic stuff but this other crap?" He gestured at the counter and made a face, "this other stuff is crazy."

Ashley said nothing, but her fingers strangled the declined coffee cup.

"So." Jason said at last. "I just wanted to say this in person, okay? That's why I came over, okay?" His eyes at first sought to capture hers and then settled once more on the gruesome mess on the counter. "This is probably illegal! Like, what? Is this someone's cat?" He shook his head. "That's not what I meant to say." He walked to the door and opened it, adding. "I think you know what I am trying to say. I'm sorry. I can't do this anymore." Jason shut the door quietly behind him.

Ashely opened and closed her lips, then, screamed as she threw the coffee cup at the door, "But I'm pregnant!"

It is likely that Jason did not hear these words as he strode rapidly toward his car and who knows what he would have done even if he had heard them? Either way, it didn't matter. There were things that Ashely could do, would do.

Ashley almost flew to her warded room and let down her hair. Three drops of blood. It was a crude doll she made all that night, and there would be a cost to pay, true, but well worth the price. Not only had she been scorned, but, and even if he did not know, even if he had not heard the words, it did not make the pregnancy all the less real.

With the darkness finished, the snare needed to be set. Ashely texted Jason, "Need to talk. Urgent"

But Jason did not text back, not that time and not the twenty times that followed it until she had no choice but to go to his workplace, enduring the look of disgust on his face when he saw her. It would be worth it, she told herself. It would be worth the current humiliation. He didn't know what was in store for him and it was true, he did not.

"Ashley." He grabbed her arm and walked with her toward the doors leading from the office where he worked. "You can't come here. You need to stop this."

Ashley said in a composed voice, "I am pregnant."

Jason stop walking for a moment took a quick look at her face and then, walked her out of the office and into the hallway. "Even if I were to believe you, this is not the place to talk about it."

Ashley offered half of a smile. "When should we talk about it? Is there a place in your busy schedule to talk about your unborn child?"

Jason knuckled his face in exasperation. "How do I even know it's mine?" He growled. "Oh don't worry, if it is, I will honor my responsibility." He ushered her toward the elevator.

"How good of you." Ashely said sweetly. "Then again, why would I want a child of yours? Maybe I will kill it instead."

Jason pushed the elevator button angrily but said nothing and Ashley suddenly threw herself against him, her arms around his waist causing him to back away, but she clung tightly. "Ashely." Jason began but just as suddenly as she had thrown herself against him did she release him, having done all that she had set out to do. The small, wrapped token had been slipped into his jacket pocket. It was done.

Ashely walked away without another word, even as Jason called out to her. All there was left to do now was wait, and so she did, the child growing big and strong within her. Two months of waiting's worth it took and then, finally, the news of the accident reached her eager ears.

A car accident it had been and Jason in the hospital broken and in a coma and who knew if he would survive?

And that is when the pain began.

Ashely woke with a smile that quickly turned into a grimace. She clutched at her midsection, almost kneading her stomach as if it were bread dough. "No." She whispered, "No."

But the drop of blood on the sheet told a different story.

"No." she whispered again, carefully getting out of bed and moving in a half crouch to her warded room. "No." She panted as she poured water into her scyring bowl, dreading what she would see. A child's face looked back at her and she almost sighed with relief until the child spoke.

"In this lifetime, I may choose." The infant said. "Times three, the pain to thee ..."

"No," Ashley whimpered.

"Yes." The baby answered with eyes solemn and dark. "... And my choice, to be free, to choose another, blessed be." And the infant's face was gone, only the reflection of Ashley's eyes in the water and the pain remained.

Wave after wave of pain struck her and she fell to her knees even as the doctors fought to save Jason's life. And save it they did and it seemed a miracle that they could. But there was no one to save Ashely as she bled that night, not even herself. For every inch Jason gained in his way back to the light, Ashely lost a little more to the dark until finally, the balance was met. Eyes glazed and unseeing, Ashely stared blankly at the ceiling, blood like a cape of guilt around her lifeless body.

So mote it be.(what is this?)

POP GOES THE ZOMBIE

THE GIRL SPRINTED FOR HER life, darting between ruined cars and overturned debris. The sound of hungry zombies was behind her and a small light, shining like a beacon of hope, shone from the window of a barricaded six-floor building just ahead.

The girl panted as she ran. Could it possibly be another survivor? But what else could the light mean? Zombies didn't light candles or use flashlights. "Please, please, please...," she whispered as she ran toward the fence that was being pulled to the side by yes, another person!

The man motioned to her with one hand while his other hand clutched a gun. The girl ran inside the enclosure and toward the door that stood open to the apartment foyer beyond. The man stopped her with his hand held out in a halting gesture and pointed the gun. "Do you speak English?"

"Y-yes," she stammered in relief, "Thank God I have found you!"

"Hm, yes," the man cryptically replied. Keeping the gun pointed in her direction, he eyed her as she walked inside of the foyer but he motioned with the gun as she went to step further inside. The girl could hear the zombies in the distance; they had her scent. It wouldn't be long before they found her.

"Have you been bitten?" the man asked from just inside of the door, the gun never wavering.

"No. No, I haven't been bitten," she responded, and she hadn't been. She didn't even know how she had managed it these past weeks. She had become separated from the group she traveled with, and when the attack came, there had been no choice, them or her. There had been no choice at all.

"Turn around," the man ordered, and she did, holding her arms up, lip quivering.

"You sure you haven't been bit?" he asked, and she could understand his fear, understand it all too well.

"I'm sure," the girl assured him. "Not even a scratch."

A bite always took, a scratch didn't always, but she had neither, and she still couldn't believe she had been so lucky.

"Take off your clothes," the man ordered curtly and even this she could understand, but it was very cold standing there in front of the open door, a door that promised warmth and shelter and hopefully some food.

"L-look," she stammered, teeth chattering with the cold and reaction, "may I please come inside? Just inside the door, you can keep the gun on me but..."

The man started to close the door eyeing her carefully, and she gave a soft and frustrated wail, "No, wait! Here. Look."

She pulled off her coat, feeling the buttons snap off in her haste. The man opened the door slightly, watching.

Her sweater came off next, along with her tee shirt. She held out her arms again, showing him. Turning. She could hear a moan in the distance, and she shivered.

"Pants," the man hissed, and she yanked her worn blue jeans off, dancing around as she kicked off her boots, almost tripping.

"Look!" she whispered frantically, first showing him one leg and then the other, "no bites!"

"All of it! Hurry!" he hissed again. She looked at him for a moment and then shucked off her bra, throwing it to the side and then slid out of the boxer briefs she had found in a deserted clothing store. She reached down and yanked off her socks and then stood naked and shook with her arms across her chest.

"Turn around, arms up," he ordered. "Bend over, legs spread."

Gritting her teeth, she did as she was told, she could understand why he was careful, especially if he had others to protect.

She could hear the moaning sounds coming closer. "No bites," she whispered, "none."

"Come on," the man held the door open, and she bent to retrieve her clothes, but he made an impatient movement with his hand, "hurry and get inside."

She grabbed her clothes and ran toward the open door which the man bolted from the inside with an elaborate mass of chains. Her stomach growled with hunger as she watched him secure the door and still naked, she followed the man past the useless elevators to the stairwell.

"You first," he grunted, and she began to climb, holding on to the guardrail as she did. She had been running for days.

She made it to the second floor of the building before she tripped, feeling the man behind her inhale sharply as she did. "Get up!" he ordered urgently.

"Please," she begged, "let me catch my breath. I'm exhausted."

"Or maybe you are sick," the man replied suspiciously, "or getting sick."

"I'm just tired. No bites. None. You can see."

"Upstairs, go. There will be time to rest when we get there. If you have enough breath to complain, you have enough breath to climb!"

When they reached the sixth floor, she waited while he unbolted the padlock and then followed him through to the hallway and then, four doors down, into the small apartment from which she had seen the light.

She stumbled toward the couch, and he let her do that much. She fell almost face forward, breathing hard, no longer shivering but sweating instead. She felt something against her hand, a cup, and sat up enough to drink from it. Cool, refreshing water. A blessing.

"Not so fast or you will sick it up," the man remarked almost conversationally.

She breathed gratefully, "Thank you. Thank you so much."

The man grunted.

The girl turned on the couch, smile ready which froze when she saw the man still held the gun aimed in her direction. She opened her mouth, but he interrupted. "I need to examine you,"

The girl closed her mouth, watching his face and eyeing the gun. She nodded.

"Lay on your back," he ordered, and she did,

sprawled out on the couch as he took his time looking. "Turn over," he instructed, and she did that as well, feeling his eyes on her as he took his time but it would be okay, it would be fine. She didn't have a single bite, not even a scratch.

"See?" she asked and started to turn over on her side facing him. "Wait!" he said, and there was something wrong with his voice but she didn't know what it was and she was so tired. She let him look; there was nothing to see, she had been lucky.

She heard him panting and a rustling of clothes then she realized that she did know what that sound was. She hitched her shoulders resentfully. Seriously? Was he really doing *that*?

She heard a gasp, and then he was beside her on the couch, and she resigned herself. It was, she supposed, a small price to pay for safety. And it was funny how many things had changed and yet, hadn't.

She let herself be turned onto her back once more, and that was when she really looked at him, really looked. He was sick, there was no doubt about it, none at all. He looked at her ruefully as he finished zipping up his jeans, coughing. "You may not have been bitten, but I was. It won't be long now."

"You bastard!" She shrieked of anger. "You let me think..."

"There is no time for this," he said as he handed her the gun.

"No time?" she managed. "And yet, you ... you ... Took time to... to ..."

She grabbed for the gun, and he let her take it, smiling to himself as she blinked away tears.

"Can you blame me?" he asked.

And she couldn't, not really, and it was funny, that. Funny how things had changed so much but hadn't, that she couldn't really blame him at all.

But that didn't stop her from pulling the trigger.

THE COOKIE LOTTERY

"The Big Cookie Disaster of 1885" happened during a busy time for women. There, Mary Ann Shad and her Anti- Slavery Society, and Abigail Becker, a heroine who was paramount in saving the lives of the master and six men of the crew of the schooner, "Conductor." One could only marvel, as one turned the pages of the newspaper, at Harriet Tubman, a conductor on the famous escape route called "The Underground Railroad or Susanna Moodie, who published fascinating journals and a book called "Roughing it in the Bush."

In the town of Campville, a small town situated between something and not very much, north of south and north enough to have snow, lived Josephine Napoleon, a woman of graying years, eccentric and rather self-absorbed, an artist, self-taught and passionate. For Josephine, it too was a busy time. It was the holiday season, and that meant cookies.

Obsessed with her art was Josephine, and perhaps that is the real reason things happened as they did or perhaps it was something else, something far more sinister.

The eccentricity of Josephine was a thing that could be excused as she was both witty and kind. Although she was known to have strong opinions so as to render her unbearable, her delightful sense of fun made you want to come to the many parties that she held for the other widows in the town. And, her saving grace was that She listened and could be counted on to be close-mouthed.

Josephine lived her life in the town of Campville and

in many ways the town itself was her life since she had, as she put it, "many oars in." It was a great surprise to everyone, including herself, when Josephine poisoned so many of the town's residents.

That the deaths included some of the most annoying women of Campville was, as Josephine was to say, "pure coincidence!"

Josephine Napoleon was not an obese woman, but she was far from slim. Asthmatic symptoms had led to an unwanted suggestion by her doctor for her to lose weight and Josephine was not pleased.

"It is insulting what the body can do to betray you," she was later to tell her friend Nora Whittle who ventured a brave greeting to Josephine as she stomped along the snow shoveled sidewalks, head down and growling, " A diet? Outrageous!"

In Josephine's house, on Josephine's counters, and every available table or surface were pans of varied types of Christmas cookies. " A veritable ticking time bomb for an impending heart attack or a stroke residing in every squashed, miss shaped or dimpled dainty," said Josephine to a certain Maryanne Stapleton, who agreed most definitely that cookies were a form of tasty evilness, this while patting her scrawny shanks as she served the tea.

At her next party and with a set will, Josephine gave away parceled cookies to her departing guests, inwardly horrified that many of her friends had the bad taste of giving her cookies as hostess gifts. Didn't they remember she was trying to get rid of *her* cookies! She had to lose weight for prescribed medical reasons, how could they be so thoughtless?

Now Josephine loved to garden, and it was a shame that she misread the label on the small bottle of slug poison. She mistook it for vanilla, and perhaps her dimming eyesight contributed to the calamity, but really, she hadn't meant to kill anyone, and it truly seemed unfair that people were so angry with her about it.

Sure, there were a few people that the town was better off without, but she hadn't caused their deaths on purpose, or so she kept telling herself as she mixed her paint and readied her canvas, dabbing her brush and painting a circle.

As Josephine painted, her mind went to a place far from where she stood, and in the back of her mind, a little voice snickered, "Aren't you glad that they are gone? What a relief!"

The other voice, a nicer voice, was quick in its soft-voiced rebuttal, "of course I am not glad. What an awful thing to have happened!"

The two voices argued back and forth, the one pointing out the benefits of a certain aggravating person's demise as the other argued for his or her virtues and sticking to the belief, quite firmly, that it was a tragedy and that was that.

Tired, hand weary and sporting a headache, Josephine stepped away from the painting and viewed it from many angles. She had not quite got the facial color correct in a few places, but otherwise, the images of her so-called, " Cookie Victims" were easily recognizable.

There was Andria Middletown, a two-faced back-stabber if there ever was one. Freeloading at parties and never returning the favor. Andria and her expensive hats. The town was too small to exclude her. And there, her pudgy hand outstretched toward a plate of Red Velvet cookies; you could almost see the sin of gluttony in her eyes. It was helped along by a touch of the deepest purple, a mauve really, on a ready mouth that almost glistened with the glossy brushes of white that suggested saliva in the drool upon her chin.

Arline Brooth.

Josephine frowned as she looked at the image of Arline. She didn't hate, Arline. You really couldn't hate Arlene, and perhaps that was one of the reasons that you almost felt compelled to do so. She was in her late sixties! She could pass for someone in their forties. And she was so nice!

In the painting, Arline Brooth sat at a table covered with a red and white patterned tablecloth on which every manner of serving dish Josephine could think of was painted, bearing a beguiling multitude of cookies.

From the simple, yet grainy looking wheat cookie to the far more detailed and visually stunning eclair, Josephine had a knack for detail.

Oatmeal raisin cookies -.a tan color made of pale yellow ochre with a touch of white and flecks of burnt umber for the raisins. A rim of burnt sienna circling the bottom of each cookie showcased that they had been slightly overbaked.

For the peanut butter cookies, Cadmium yellow with a touch of titanium white and yellow ochre to create a very pale sand and for the nuts, inside a rich, deep yellow ochre with a touch of burnt sienna.

Josephine examined the painting; her eyes squinting thoughtfully, and her unintended victims stared back.

There, her son Cornelius, behind the stacked cinnamon crisps, that had been a bit of a toughie; the light had been dreadful. Cornelius, who was an attendee of parties and little else. Josephine's nostrils flared briefly, eleven hours of labor and the fruits of it utterly useless no matter what the effort. She was grateful that her husband, Marcus, rest his soul, had not lived to see the day of his son's reckoning. The day their son, Cornelius met Rebecca.

And there she stood, wildfire hair streaming across guileless eyes. She does not eat a cookie, no, not her! But there, there is her hand sneaking a strawberry wafer into her stole.

Josephine stepped back and let her chin drop to her ample bosom. It had obviously been an accident; the police said that is was. Why would she have wanted her son to die? Even if he *had* been a major disappointment. No. It surely had been an accident, no matter how fortuitous. Josephine lifted her chin. Perhaps *happy* was not the exact word she would use to describe what she was feeling about the deaths of so many people, perhaps the word *relief* would make for a better fit, for there was no denying it, the town was simply better off without them.

Muina Flembaker's twitchy, perpetually self-serving eyes stared at her from behind a plateful of Cardinum Kisses, and Alice White shoved a Date Square into a stern and disapproving mouth. A plate full of lamp black lava cookies with a dollop of ivory colored icing tempted Florence Bellow, and heaven only knew, *nobody* was going to miss *her!*

There was not a single cookie in Josephine's kitchen; all had been confiscated by the police. Josephine was glad that the cookies were gone. The lack of temptation was refreshing, and she dined sensibly on salad and a simple rice dish before retiring for the evening on her couch. She fell asleep, and the painting of the many faces of the newly departed gazed down upon her as she snored.

Perhaps it was the fact that Josephine had been aggravated by the suggestion to lose weight or, perhaps it was the deaths due to her cookies, or maybe, just maybe, it was that the failing background light as the sun disappeared behind a cloud caused her to take off her eyeglasses.

Perhaps, and this was also whispered, it had something to do with all of those things but in the words of Gertrude Dandle, a survivor, "It sure does seem strange that she would paint herself onto the canvas." Gertrude was much given to pulp mysteries, and she did have a point, but Josephine's death was deemed as accidental as the ones that she had caused. But the fact that Josephine had poisoned herself with house plant tablets, and as it turned out, had an allergy to plant food did seem odd. It appeared to many people in the town of Campville to be just desserts, but of course, none of them said it out loud because that would have been tasteless.

Josephine's estranged daughter kept the painting at first but it made her uneasy, and she donated it to the Campville museum who didn't want it but accepted it anyway. They put the painting into storage where it had languished for some years before it was eventually purchased by Philbus Antwater who bought the painting at an auction and it is his words that are perhaps the most appropriate an ending.

The irony of faces from a canvas staring down at the woman who painted it while she died had not been lost on Philibus. "It's all about cookies," he said when he was asked why he had bought it. "In the end," he added, as he straightened the painting carefully, patting it with affection. "it's all about cookies."

THE APPLE

Summary: The Apple is a post-apocalyptic love story about survival and hope. It illustrates the strength of character needed to make a personal sacrifice to ensure a better future or any future at all.

I PUT SOME GREEN IN THE whatsit and it makes a whirring sound. Adding some of the other stuff, I yawn as I watch it blend and bubble. My boyo Tommybobby brought me minty leaves he found outside, and I add one in. This is going to taste delicious. I hope.

"Guess what I found?" Tommybobby says when he comes in from where he was, his hands behind his back.

I yawn again and shrug, pretending I don't care.

"Oh, don't even," he laughs, all happy and tongue out. "I know you want to know."

He's right of course, I do want to know. Tommybobby is one of the best scavengers I have ever met. But it is first light and I am not a first light kind of girlie.

"You want me to guess, I am guessing."

Tommybobby smiles. "Yes, you get three."

Tommybobby is a pretty boyo, hardly any sores or warts and most of his parts are in the right places. He has the bluest eye I've ever seen.

I just sort of stand there. I'm sure I have that look I always have at first light. I have hair and it's always messy when I wake up. Tommybobby says it makes me look delicious.

"Wellhey?" He says and I sigh inwardly. Turning the whatsit off, I grab a holder, pour the stuff, and take a sip. I pucker up and my eyes pinch shut at the taste. Too much green and maybe the leaf wasn't the best idea.

"Jennysally." He makes the last half of my name one long "eeeee" sound and I force another sip, trying to wake up enough to play.

"Okay. Is it alive?" I mumble as I chew on some bits of minty leaf.

I can feel Tommybobbie's face brighten, even with my back turned.

"No!" He pants in that way he has. "Two more."

"Want some stuff?" I reach for another holder, thinking and stalling.

"No, I'm cold." His ears are all flip floppy and perk. "Wellso? Guess!"

I turn around and can't help smile a little, he is just too crawly. "Okay. Did it *used* to be alive?"

"You think with your mouth," he says and he is too right. But Tommybobby has a way of finding dead things that makes me the envy of everybody. They say he can find things that can't be found and it's true. Girlies rub up on him but he does nothing about that.

"No!" He laughs and his hands are still behind his back so I play along and snatch at his arm. He pulls away, snorting. "Nuh. Third guess."

Even standing I have to look up at him, balancing on my good foot; he's so tall. His eye is sparkling. Whatever he has must be good.

"Where did you find it?" That answer might give me some clue. "Were you scouting in the blank place again?"

And he may have been, he is brave like that. Me, I would never go. I don't even want to look.

"Nuh." He shakes his head and laughs again. Something makes a noise when he does.

"What is that?" I reach but he pulls away again.

"Third guess!"

It's too early for this but its love that I even try.

"Burny crap?" It's the best I can do after only one holder of stuff. I'm kind of hoping it is burny crap. We need some.

"Nuh!" He sort of hops up and down and puts his hands in front of him and lets me see.

"Oh," I say, and I can't help but be downlow. It's another kid thing. A something that has lots of colors and it is sort of round. We can't eat it and we can't burn it but Tommybobby, he likes his kid things. We have a whole bunch of them.

"Wellhey." He bends over to look into my face and I know what he's thinking with this kid thing. And maybe he's right. I have been very tired and maybe I am growing another pup and just maybe this one will stay alive. Mostly they don't and then it's off to MissMolly and then we have stew.

"Hey?" Tommybobby says all gentle and I know he is wishing but maybe I just can't make one that stays breathing like that bitch, Cindymindy. She has three, for fug's sake. Then again, they all have tails.

I kind of hunch over while he is playing with the kid thing and I am watching and I am thinking.

"Heyo," I say finally and he looks up at me. "Maybe I just can't. You know?" I look down at my holder.

He stops playing and stands close and I breath him

right in. "Heyo," he says gently. "Nuh. Nuh. If you can't, you can't."

I whirl away from him and pour another holder of stuff. "Lookyou," I say. "All this kid stuff? I know. Okay? Don't."

"So?" he shouts and I turn fast cuz Tommybobby doesn't yell. "So?" He's yelling and I'm standing with my mouth open but it's not me he's yelling at.

I look at what he's looking at and it's my ex boyo standing at the mouth of the cave. This won't be good.

My ex, Briandanny, is a complete hole and what I ever saw in him, I don't know. He was never happy to see me move in with Tommybobby and says it when we see him but he has never once come here to say it.

"What do you say, Briandanny?" Tommybobby is making a growling sound that is both scary and sexy and makes me feel pink.

"Heyuh?" Briandanny is holding both of his hands out in a "don't eat me" gesture. I have to respect it, even though I always thought his leg meats would go good with dumplings.

"Whata?" Tommybobby growls and I touch his arm and feel warm.

See, Briandanny was my first sex thing and it wasn't great. He has boy *and* girl parts and I was never sure what to do with the boy parts to begin with, let alone the other thing. I put a bottle in it once, just to see if I could, and it slid in just like that. He never stopped griefing me about it either.

"There is a meeting at the town place, just wanting to say."

Both Tommybobby and I sort of stare because we don't have meetings at the town place unless it is a kill thing or a who did something.

"A meeting?" I say, confused.

"Yuh!" Briandanny says with excitement and I can see he isn't thinking about the bottle thing and Tommybobby isn't thinking anymore about hurting Briandanny. I think.

"Huh!" Tommybobby says and he grabs my arm.

I almost fall over but hook a claw into his arm so I don't. "Masks, get em!"

And he's still glaring at Briandanny but yuh, you can see it, nothing will happen. Even so, I sniff to make sure before I go. Tommybobby pats me and then I see Briandanny glaring and I think how stupid boyos are.

I grab both masks and we follow Briandanny out of the cave and down the steps and through the digging part and past farm and by then, I see others like us. Some are wearing masks and others, like dumbass Briandanny, are not wearing masks. And that's just stupid but I can't change the world.

We get to the town place which is an actual house that people live in. We let Davidbenny and his girlie Barbyjan live in it because they can read bookish, and we made farm because the book told us how. Farm doesn't grow much except for mushrooms but they are tasty unless they kill you.

People are standing or sitting and we find a place, Tommybobby and I. Briandanny looked as if he was going to squat beside us until Tombobby gave him a look out of that eye of his that would have killed Brian-danny if things worked like that.

I sit there beside my boyo and lean on him, feeling kind of sick. Maybe I am growing a pup or maybe it was the leaf I drank. I am not sure but Tommybobby is pretty good at what he finds; like I said, he is the best scavenger I ever met. I touch my stomach. Maybe? Thing is, I don't really want another one although I have never told Tommybobby this. I have had three now and each time it was harder to take it to MissMolly. I kept the last one 'til it was almost spoiled and she gave me hellfire about it too.

Seems like almost everybody did at the time; except for Tommybobby, who just let me pretend and let me keep it for as long as I needed to, even with it smelling bad.

I look over to where Cindymindy is sitting with her three. Tails or no tails, they look pretty crawly to me and I feel all downlow. Tommybobby puts an arm around me and holds me close and I breathe, just breathe.

There's a buzzy sound and we all look at Davidben-ny as he walks to the ledge thing he calls a porch. "Listen!" He calls out and his girlie Barbiejan crawls out to crouch beside him. She is posh for all she doesn't have much in the way of bones and is kind of sloshy. And I really am trying to pay attention because we don't have meetings usually, but I keep looking at Cindymindy's pups, with them all holding onto each other's tails and I'm thinking how maybe I do want one after all.

Tommybobby always knows what I'm thinking and he gives me a squeeze and a lick on the cheek.

"Listen," Davidbenny says again, "I found a book thing and it's something we all should know."

Oh. Another book thing. Well, it's not like book things aren't important because we find out stuff this way, but I'm tired and didn't have first food and my stomach is making sounds.

I tune out and just rest against Tommybobby, knowing he will tell me what the book thing is about later, but he gives me a little shake and keeps nodding his chin at Davidbenny. I know he wants me to listen, so I do.

"Barbiejan and I have read this over and over about these things called," he spells it out, "Vit a mins."

I look at Tommybobby but I can see he is listening really careful as both of his ears are turned sharply toward Davidbenny.

Davidbenny says, "These Vitamins are important things and we need to find them. I know too many of you are losing pups and it says in the book thing that all girlies need to be eating them." He frowns. "Well, swallowing them or drinking them."

Someone calls out, "Where we get these vit things?"

Barbiejan speaks up from where she is all sloshed, "We find them in stores."

There is a quiet, of course there is. These stores are past the blank place and nobody ever goes there anymore, masks or no masks. The few who have made it back don't live long and you can't eat them they are so sored up.

A few from the crowd get up and leave. I want to but Tommybobby holds me in place.

"It says these vitamins will help us grow healthy-wise. And for girlies, helps them grow healthy pups." Davidbenny is raising his voice now and you can tell he means what he says, but what are we supposed to do about that? We can't go to stores. I turn my head to say as much to Tommybobby and freeze when I see the look in his eye. I can smell what he is thinking.

"Nuh!" I nudge him hard. "You don't think about it! Nuh!"

There is more stuff about how to get to the stores and wearing some stuff and better masks but I am shaking hard because I can see Tommybobby nodding like a hole and I want to hit him or hug him or drag him home to the cave and tie him up because I know he is thinking about trying it. I know he is!

"Just one of these vitamins a day, even if it's just for the girlies ... "

And Davidbenny and Barbiejan are still talking and Tommybobby is still nodding and I can't feel my hands and my hair hurts and I realize I have been grabbing on to it and twisting. I pant and send it into Tommybobby and he looks at me.

Tommybobby is quiet as we head home, he doesn't even say anything to Briandanny who keeps looking at me that way and sniffing.

In the cave, I am shaking Tommybobby and he is not saying anything but smiling at me the way he knows how. We have sex and I cry but I know he is leaving anyway.

I tell him I don't have a pup growing but he pats

my stomach and he pets my hair and, come first light, I don't have to even wake up to know he's gone. He left his new kid thing beside me and I scream and go to throw it but then I don't. I hug it instead.

He is the best scavenger I know. This is what I tell myself as my stomach gets bigger. Tommybobby is the best scavenger I know.

MY KRAKEN

IT WAS A SMALL KRAKEN as Kraken's go, but lithe and in good health. Its barnacled tentacles were moist and gelatinous, and it slithered up the ladder that clung to the blue and white striped pontoon boat.

Coiled within one of its limbs was a small shell which it held protectively. The Kraken's blinking eyes expelled lake water, opening and closing rapidly; almost coquettishly.

The pontoon rocked with the Kraken's weight, but the creature held firmly, inching itself across the top of the pontoon's rails and sending fishing rods flying. It flailed a tentacle with determination, its desired objective in view.

"Hello," it screeched, "I am a scary Kraken." And it was.

The Kraken thumped to the deck in some exhaustion and pushed itself slowly toward the front of the boat. Krakens do not climb particularly well, being much like an octopus in build and they are not land creatures, although they may spend time there if properly motivated. No, a Kraken is a water beast; graceless on a hard surface but like a ballerina in the water. Many a Kraken have made a name for themselves in this area, if only amongst themselves.

The heat from the sun made the Kraken quiver, but it did not waver in its destination. An excited huffing noise could be heard heaving through its coarsely hair covered gills and it almost lost its grip on its prize.

The Kraken made sure that one of its suction cups kept hold of its treasure, wriggled and crawled as fast as it was able and at last, gasping, pressed its weight against the boy who held one hand on the steering wheel and the other hand outstretched.

The Kraken's form began to melt and lapsed into that of a large black dog with the shell held carefully in its mouth.

"Good boy, Brutus," the boy said, "but I said, get the BELL, not the shell..."

The Weredog's tail drooped. He laid the shell down and looked sheepish as his boy smiled, then laughed as he hugged his beloved pet.

SASHA BROOK

Sasha Brook had glorious, honey colored hair that was shiny and full of natural highlights. It was simply gorgeous hair... and as Amy the Vampire mumbled, "I just can't kill her, that hair, that incredible mane of hair!"... and the other Vampires nodded in agreement as they gathered around the entranced and sleep induced Sasha Brook. It was true, you didn't often see hair like that.

Sasha Brook, at the tender age of sixteen, had already developed a mature, ripe figure but it was her eyes, those honey- tinged, hazel eyes with their pin pricks of green, that caused another two Vampires to drop out of the auction. Sasha really did have lovely eyes, they were clear and innocent and heck, you could feel that darned sweetness even with the girl asleep and her eyes shut.

Hazel grumbled as she left Sasha's darkened bedroom, "I just can't!" She took her friend Suzette with her and they shook their heads at the sorrow of it all, "that nose...," they murmured to each other, and resigned not to bid on Sasha, the two saddened Vampires flitted off, determined to find someone else, an uglier someone, who was ready to die.

"Bye," waved Bart, an elderly Vampire who raptly petted Sasha's hair as it lay spread across her pillow. Amy gave a wave to the two departing Vampires and then frowning, rearranged Sasha's locks where Bart had tousled them. The two Vampires locked eyes and Bart slowly turned one thumb up.

He would bid.

Simon leered from his corner lusting after the sleeping

beauty but held his thumb still indecisive. While Leona, whining Leona, whimpered, "Why does she have to be so pretty?" She stared forlornly at the sleeping Sasha's face her thumb held in abeyance. "I always wanted to look like that. I tried so hard. I worked out, I drank water, I got highlights and a nose job and..."

Bart interrupted, "She has an aneurysm, her ribbon will soon be cut no matter what we do or," he nodded in Amy's direction, "not do."

And he was right of course, Sasha Brooke was going to die peacefully in her sleep, and that was another thing. It wouldn't even hurt! It would never be something that a Vampire could even feel good about. So what if one of them cheated The Reaper? It wasn't something that one could say later, "well, the poor little thing was in so much pain, it really was better this way!"

"...and she is a girl scout," volunteered Amy, somehow becoming Sasha Brook's defender and Leona moaned and edged toward the open window.

Amy added, giving a pointed look at both Bart and Simon, "She does **CRAFTS!**"

"But..." Bart faltered and Simon looked away, "She *is* going to die, it›s not like, I mean.." Amy looked at Bart sternly and the older Vampire looked away feeling as embarrassed as if he had been caught poaching on a toddler.

"So young," Amy all but whispered as she smoothed Sasha Brook's hair, "she hasn't even had a first kiss."

"Pure," coughed Leona uneasily, "she could be a Disney character."

Pedro flew into the room, late as always, and did a double take as he peered down at Sasha Brook who gave a small sigh in her sleep that sounded like the cooing of a dove. Pedro turned troubled eyes toward his fellow blood drinkers and said, "Madre de dios! She is an angel..." he stroked her cheek and lifted one of her hands in his larger ones and planted a kiss on her palm, "an angel," he repeated and down went his thumb.

Bart, a hand wringing gargoyle, slumped and then turned his thumb down as well. "I've changed my mind," he admitted. "One rarely finds such a fine creation and I cannot bear to have a hand in this. I cannot even bring myself to look upon the winner."

Bart walked over to Sasha Brook's open window under the approving gaze of Amy who sat on the corner of the bed beside the sleeping Sasha Brook. Simon still in his corner, glowered from beneath scowling eyebrows while Pedro wept and muttered to himself in Spanish.

Leona floated over to the window, turned her thumb down and whined, "It isn't fair..." and was gone in a flash, Bart, hot on her heels and without so much as a backward glance or farewell, fled from the room which left Amy, Simon and Pedro.

"I cannot!" Pedro declared, touching the sleeping girl's cheek, "I will not! She is far too lovely," as he stepped into shadow and departed. Amy stroked the lovely girl's hair and Simon finally left his corner. He wandered the room making furtive glances at Sasha like a depressed voyeur.

It was a pretty room, painted in several shades of

green with a shelf devoted to ribbons and trophies and another to Beanie Babies and pretty shells. Framed pictures of family and friends adorned the walls along with posters of fairies and elves.

Simon looked at Amy who said calmly, "it needn't be at our hands, let her die as nature intended. Let us leave this child unsullied and untarnished, in death as she was in life.

Simon glided softly over to where Amy sat weaving a small loose braid into Sasha Brook's hair. He shifted uncomfortably and blurted "I have a reputation..."

Amy replied kindly. "You have my oath that no one would ever know should you choose to spare this beautiful child."

Simon gazed reluctantly at Sasha Brook, at her small, slim fingers crossed daintily across a green, leaf-patterned comforter. "Spare? There is no help for it, she *is* going to die."

"Yes, but she would at least be untouched...

"Yes, yes," Simon responded impatiently, "unsullied, untarnished, I get it, it's just..." he sighed, "Look, it's fine, whatever," he sneered an almost authentic sneer this time, "Who wants pie filling when there is lard to be found?"

Amy frowned and paused in her braiding, "What in hell does that even mean?"

Simon ventured a hand and then withdrew it without touching Sasha Brook. "It means nothing," he shook his head slightly, "nothing at all." Without further ado, Simon exited Sasha Brook's bedroom and Amy gave a relieved sigh.

Later that week the obituary for Sasha Brook spoke of her virtues and accomplishments, and the tragedy of the unexpected aneurysm. However, the article did leave out one important detail. The funeral director was later to say to his assistant as the coffin was closed after the service... "We sure was lucky to find a wig in time for the viewin'!"

Sasha Brook did indeed die a peaceful death but she did so without a strand of hair on her head. For as Amy put it at as she sat humming and shaving, "bald she came into this world, so she shall leave it."

It seemed enough justification for Sasha Brook truly did have lovely hair.

SALTWATER

SALTWATER WAS A DARK FEY. He was dark in nature, but more than that, Saltwater was dark in spirit. Too Dark. He was so dark that Saltwater's parents had practically given up. They could only wish that, now that their son was old enough, he would just flit, shimmer, or just Goddess knows, slink away and go be dark somewhere else other than his bedroom.

Saltwater's parents, Salacious and his terrifying wife Lemon-drop, were at their wits end. There was a circle of salt in front of their son's bedroom, which prevented them from entering or even knocking. Once caught in that stuff, that horrid warding stuff, a dark fey had to count every grain. It was just plain annoying and was the last straw, so to speak.

How their son had even managed to get the blasted salt in the first place was a puzzle, but it was the sheer nastiness of it that hurt! If he had done it to anyone else, Salacious and Lemon-drop could have at least have been proud, but to do it them? To his own parents?

From the very beginning, Saltwater had been difficult. He had even been difficult to conceive. With great reluctance, since he had a rather jealous nature, Salacious had averted his blood red eyes as his wife took advantage of a mortal late one night after too many bottles of dew and too many arguments. His sperm had just not been vicious enough and Salacious just had to accept the fact, since he did want a child - a little girl to spoil with pretend poison parties, or a little boy to play bat ball. Salacious had drawn the line at the mortal's wife raising the infant, but of course he had lost that battle as well.

"Our son will be a changeling," Lemon-drop had firmly declared, adding as the final clincher, "I don't have time to change cobwebs."

Perhaps this had been the start of it all, but Lemon-drop, nineteen years later, still held her ground as the arguments continued. She refused to believe that her son's behavior had anything to do with the caregiving given by a mortal - until a boggle could be found to replace Saltwater in his crib at the Johnson's house. She denied any and all culpability.

Even when Salacious and Lemon-drop heard the wails of horror when Bill and Sue Johnson discovered the boggle, it had brought little pleasure. For as soon as Lemon-drop held her toddler in her furred arms, the child had refused to glare at her, but smiled instead. It had been horrifying to say the least.

A Pooka who specialized in behavioral modification had been brought in immediately. Saltwater did learn to scowl effectively, but Salacious had always wondered about his son. As much as he wanted to nurture his child's dark magic, Saltwater had kept asking for ponies and making flowers sparkle until Salacious wanted to slap the boy.

He hadn't, of course. Salacious always maintained, loudly if necessary, that he would stand by his son, no matter what he was. Even as the young Saltwater drew rainbows instead of dripping gore in kindergarten class, or later in middle school, when he had brought a puppy home to the hidden grove. In the end, the puppy had been named Fred, and Salacious and Lemon-drop averted their eyes when Saltwater taught Fred to fetch sparkly pink tennis balls.

"It doesn't matter!" Lemon-drop wept tears of acid, leaving an attractive trail of seared flesh on her cheeks. "He is our son."

Fred became a fine and loyal dog, with loving eyes. It was off putting, but again, Salacious and Lemon-drop stood by their son, even when Fred rescued a mortal from an ogre. Commiserations came from all over, offered from the neighboring fey. Salacious and Limewater nodded their heads and even tried a few well-meant tips.

"You must douse the child in a stagnant pond. It worked with my niece when she started painting her nails. "

"Stick him in a volcano for a while. That will do the trick."

And so on, but nothing really worked. Saltwater eventually did stop smiling, which should have been a good thing, but somehow wasn't.

By the time that Saltwater started high school, he had more than an effective scowl, but it was not the right kind of scowl. It was a dissatisfied scowl, and not the scowl of pleasure that one would surely expect from a young fey with advantages.

Saltwater no longer sketched pictures of happy kittens, it was true. His drawing pad was filled with appropriate renderings of death and destruction but there was something... lacking. There was something ... off. It was as if even a scribble of a burnt building or his rather good portrait of a screaming pixie drowning in oil was somehow poignant, with a pathos that was disconcerting.

Aunt Magdela's suggestion that Saltwater be placed in an institution was not met with favor, and she had been sent flying with a burst of flame for suggesting it, but still...

On a Samhain night, Salacious eyed his son in his bright, orange tuxedo and hoped for the best. Saltwater had clutched the required bitterroot corsage in a cast off beetle shell, ready to hand to the young hag who had agreed to be his date. Salacious and Lemon-drop had taken pictures and waved, but eyed each other as the youngsters climbed into the rat pulled carriage limo. Their concerns were justified when Saltwater slunk home, (and not in a good way), before the moon had even set.

"She is just so ugly," Saltwater whined to his parents as an explanation.

"But ...but, she is a Hag, son," Salacious had stuttered. "She is supposed to be."

She was in fact, quite seriously ugly, and Salacious snuck glances when his wife wasn't looking. *That wart, hell yeah.*

"And she is really, really disgusting!" Lemon-drop had added encouragingly, but to no avail. Somehow the young Hag's ugly features were not attractive to their son. He moped off, accompanied by a charmed Fred the dog who did not age, but had remained cute and puppy-like for far, far, far too long.

Salacious and Lemon-drop pretended to ignore the pop music pounding from their son's room, its door closed against them.

And now, this salt business. All because Lemon-drop had brought home pamphlets about hex camp!

"You will find this utterly mangling!" Lemon-drop coaxed, trying to sound cool by using current teen jargon. "Look, read here." She said, unfolding the pamphlet. "You can even bring home a jinx!"

"What do you say, son?" Salacious asked as Saltwater stood there, refusing to meet their eyes or to even look at the itinerary.

"You don't want me," Saltwater said. "You never did."

"That is not true," Lemon-drop protested.

"It is," argued Saltwater. "You are always comparing me to the seed giver!" He shook his shiny, black hair that rippled down past his dimpled chin.

"You wouldn't say that if you saw the Johnson guy, I tell you. He had really blue eyes and well-formed lips. It was…well, it was terrible is what it was! But we so wanted a child, and your father…"

Salacious looked away as he usually did, trying not to think about it. He had heard this story too many times.

Saltwater apparently had as well, as he scoffed (And not in a good way), "Ma, I have heard this story before!"

"Well," retorted Lemon-drop, "It is still true, the mortal was gorgeous."

"You know," Saltwater sneered, "You have told me

this story so many times, that I am starting to think you enjoyed it!"

This remark rendered his mother silent with shock and prompted a slight nod of agreement from Salacious, who couldn't help himself. It was true. There were times it really did seem that way.

True or not, he came to the defense of his wife, saying, "You apologize to your mother this instant, I am sure she would have preferred... something, a little less..."

"What? A little less what?" Lemon-drop screeched defensively.

"Oh come on. Admit it. You liked it. Look at dad, he knows what I mean. Are you two getting a divorce?"

Salacious opened his beaky mouth, but not a sound emerged. Lemon-drop looked between her husband and her frustrating offspring. "Of course we are not getting a divorce! Whatever makes you ask that?"

Saltwater crossed his arms, an expression of smug, superior sourness in his piercing, blue eyes.

"You think I haven't heard you guys fighting? You think I can't put two and two together? I don't look like him." he motioned and sneered at his father who felt his balding pate prickle at his son's audaciousness. "And I am nothing like the other fey! Am I adopted?"

"What?" Lemon gasped at the same time that Salacious, his patience level exceeded, grabbed his son by the front of his Bee Gees tee shirt and squawked, "We have argued over you, you little snot, before you were a glimmer of mud in your mother's eyeball!"

Lemon-drop quickly added, "Your real mother! Me!

Hello? And listen, mister, there is nothing wrong with being a changeling!"

Saltwater looked unconvinced.

"Son, son," Salacious entreated, "You are my spawn, no matter how it came about."

"And you should have seen the boggle we found to put in your place—"

Saltwater cut off his mother's words, "I have been hearing that story since I was a brat. You should have just kept the boggle if you liked him so much!"

With that, Saltwater stomped to his room and slammed the door behind him with a mighty bang.

Salacious looked at his wife, who stared back in accusation.

"Yeah, that helped!" she snarled.

"Gnarling!" but his attempt at sweet talk failed, and that night, it was the couch for him.

It was the very next day that Lemon-drop discovered the circle of salt in front of her son's door. Salacious woke to the sound of his wife shrieking.

"Saltwater, you clean up this mess this instant!" Lemon-drop yelped, trying not to look at the damned stuff. "This is a new low, and don't think I won't tell your father."

"He's not my father!" Saltwater screamed.

Salacious rushed to his wife's side and she hurriedly covered her husband's eyes with her hand.

His leathery wings stretched taught in distress. "What is it?

"Salt," Lemon-drop hissed. "The handsome little bastard poured salt on the floor."

"What?" Salacious gasped. "Where? How?"

"I don't know how," Lemon-drop replied, eyes averted, a slight bit of color coming to her cheeks in a blush.

"It's his damned mortal blood, don't even try to deny it!"

Lemon-drop pulled her husband away from the salted floor, "Not in front of the offspring!"

"No. He has gone too far." Salacious pulled his wing free from his wife's grasp. "This is your fault. All of it. You wanted a cub!"

Lemon-drop gasped, "You wanted a whelp, you did!"

"Yes, I did," roared Salacious, "but you couldn't even have the decency to choose someone suitably unattractive."

"Not this again!" Lemon-drop yelled, hands covering her pointed ears. "I was drunk!"

"That's what you always say. As if it were some kind of excuse. Admit it, you acted like a succubus."

"You take that back!" Lemon-drop howled.

"I will not! I almost have to wonder if you even hated it as much as you say you did."

"Oh, really?" Lemon-drop placed her hands on her hips. "Just what are you trying to imply."

Salacious spat the word. "You are a pervert!"

"Oh!"

"You know it's true! And you left him there for almost a year, no wonder we have problems!"

Lemon-drop's bottom lips quivered, "It isn't true... I...told you..."

"Yes, you told me alright. You didn't feel like raising a baby, so why have one in the first place? Why? Admit it, you liked that Johnson guy!"

"No!"

Unnoticed by either, Saltwater watched from his slightly opened bedroom door.

"Yes, you did. Do. Still do. When was the last time we frolicked?"

Lemon-drop dripped oozing tears.

"You liked the hair, didn't you?" Salacious furiously accused, years of resentment rising to the surface like delicious scum to the top of a bewitched pool. "And his blue eyes and his dimples."

"I did not!" Lemon-drop sobbed.

"You did!" Salacious continued maliciously. "You think I don't know why you left the whelp there for so long? So you could..."

"Don't say it!"

"Watch!" continued her fed up husband.

There was a silence.

"Dad?" came Saltwater's voice from his bedroom.

Salacious huffed, and Lemon-drop turned tear filled eyes toward her son, who stepped over the salt as if it were not laying there in its warding, grainy way. Lemon-drop shook her head; her son was just so mortal at times ...

"Mom? Dad? Listen."

The next day, an enchanted and attractively dressed Lemon-drop knocked on the door of the Johnson's house. Mr. Johnson opened the door and looked between the woman and the tall young man who stood by her side.

"May I help you?" asked Mr. Johnson pleasantly.

Lemon-drop cleared her throat and Saltwater fidgeted nervously. "Ian? I would like to introduce you to your son."

THIS ISLAND,
BARNEY TEMPLETON

BARNEY TEMPLETON DID HAVE A bad case of the Fidgets, but the truth was, the Fidgets had a bad case of Barny Templeton. One had to almost turn a deep shade of Mauve! Oh, that Barney. Him and his ways. A ten-year-old boy. Really? This was the best they could do? The bumps and the thuds and the loud, frustrated screaming was bad enough, but the indifferent attention to hygiene made one thing certain – the Fidgets lived in a bad neighborhood. Children and their undeveloped development! It was enough to make one turn into the shape of a starfish, with or without pods.

The Fidgets had overshot, the aim being that of a thirteen-year-old female. The hormones were the thing, making for a rich soup from which all Fidgets could sup. It was that soup that was missing from the island that was Barney Templeton.

There would be a soup of a different flavor in the future but until then, the host, Barney, at the tender age of ten years, made for a bland and barren landscape with only the odd viral flavor to make things tasty.

But, once landed, a Fidget was bound unless the host was to meet its demise and only then would it be possible to cast off once more, in hope for a serendipitous landing.

But that day was not come and nor was the soup. And so, The Fidgets waited, living as they did, on their unsatisfactory host.

To Barney or not to Barney had become the top debate among The Fidgets and the eternal question of why they had landed on a juvenile of the specious, heatedly discussed.

In a fit of pique, first lieutenant - side mate, X7 plucked at a flaxen leg segment, which caused a change in the pheromones of young 24orb, who in its humiliation, chose to discorporate, which was a shame. Not only was 24orb sorely missed, but its action caused a reaction that started a war.

One day, on a day much like any other day, Bottom-Half chewed on one of his pseudopods, not thinking about Barney but that of Phyliss, Bottom-half's side-mate. It wasn't that he didn't feel a positronic wave when he thought of her. It had just been so long between pairings. It was use- it or lose it, and he had started losing pieces of himself several Barny Templeton heartbeats ago. As to why were they riding around on a ten-year-old child? That was the question for the theologians, not a regular Fidget like himself. He thought of the way X7's leg looked when it plucked it. That leg. Oh, that leg. So delicate a morsel.

"Sludge," Bottom-half motioned to his Imp.

'Glymph," Sludge responded.

Grimstalk, out for a stroll, gritted his pincers and a drop of ooze dripped onto the back of Barney's neck, who swiped at it with a careless hand.

Bottom-half tossed an arm at Grimstalk who caught it with a vapor of surprise. "?" it asked. Bottom-half purred, and then, looked at X7 whose fronds were undulating as Barney Templeton took off on his skateboard, frequently falling and shaking the universe as he did.

Grimstalk sketched Bottom-half a grin, gave a nod

and appeared next to X7 who extruded a startled shell. Grimstalk motioned in calmness, and X7 eased a cautious appendage in its direction only to re-erect its shell as Grimstalk offered the arm. X7 turned several shades of different colors, grew a sudden tail and then sent a burst of annoyed ammonia behind it as it backed away, to be swallowed by the colony, disappearing into the jellied mass.

Sludge the Imp gave an admonishing burble. Grimstalk offered the limb back to Bottom-half who quivered in guilty negation. Grimstalk tossed the arm to the Imp who promptly absorbed it, growing several nodules in the process.

Bottom-half watched as the legs of X7 vanished, briefly considered losing another appendage but decided against it. Marriage was hard, but the magic would come again, of that he was sure. Thinking about something was one thing but doing it was another and so caught up was he in in his thoughts that he didn't feel Grimstalk shaking against him as The Invader suddenly invaded.

And *they* had limbs to spare.

The demise of 24orb had caused a rift, and even Barney the child felt the change. Heat came first and then armies of greyish orbs, each multiple cluster sporting multiple legs, each leg covered in suction cups and oozing a slimy trail. One could taste it, this difference that was wrong, and the urge was to retreat, not an option really, unless of course, Barney, the host, should die which had suddenly become an issue in question.

Then, of course, it was abandon ship and move to a better neighborhood.

It was, in the opinion of some Fidgets, the proper course of action to take although they kept this to themselves as en masse, the majority of the Fidgets chose to fight alongside Barney Templeton. He was *their* host, child or not. And fight The Invader Barney did, and with great determination. The Fidgets were impressed, as they sat or flickered, forgotten as they were, accordion-sorted out of the path of The Invader, who pressed forward with a determination dictated by the need for the annihilation of Barney Templeton.

"Why, though? Why this invasion? " The Fidgets clicked at each other in confusion. Was it because Barney was youthful? Many of The Fidgets believed this to be the case but was this the real reason and if so, was it enough of a reason?

The invader was strong. The host was weakening. If there were Fidgets who secretly rejoiced that they might find a more respectable host after Barney's death, they kept this opinion to themselves. The popular argument was that Barney's lack of maturity was not an acceptable reason for the attack and that the age of the host was a moot point anyway as the host would mature, given time.

Bottom-half joined the Fight for The Host movement, Phyliss at his side, magic restored and sporting new pustules to prove the point. A weapon-wielding X7 who had turned female for the battle sported waving, feathery leg fronds, enough to make any Fidget quiver with lust.

The host, sickened and weak as he was, continued with a battery of negotiators. At first, peace appeared possible, but alas, The Invader was greedy and talks failed as its ambition grew.

There was hope that some truce between The Invader and The Fidgets might be accomplished. But The Invader, blind and deafened to all entreaty, simply went and absorbed the peace-seeking Fidgets, turning them into drones, or worse, breeders, to the horror and shame of many a parent Fidget. Attempts at rescue were futile as a transformed Fidget became an Invader clone and forgot about itself entirely.

The battle was a great one, and many tales were told of the bravery of fallen Fidgets, long after the war was concluded. The tale of Barney's Bone Marrow was a sad one and was made popular by the band, NMO, and achieved great commercial success.

On the Barney side of things, a veritable slew of hazardous waste was thrown at The Invader, which caused many a Fidget to question whether Barney was intent on self-destruction. But no, it seemed as if chemical warfare was aimed solely at The Invader, while simultaneously causing harm to the host, which didn't make a lot of sense but, which at that point, hardly mattered as the host was dying anyway.

But it was Grimstalk, Sludge, the Imp at the ready, that really made a difference in the end, the note that turned the oozing tide. With quick-witted accuracy, Grimstalk was able to decode a section of the invader's defense, and that was when all hell broke loose.

"More code, more code ..." Grimstalk clicked and clacked, finger-nubs working furiously at deciphering. The Invader was as clever as it was sneaky, hiding throughout the host's body, and creating havoc where it could. Several parts of the host had been removed entirely, causing further weakness for The Invader to exploit.

Bottom-half, hand in hand in hand with Phyliss, made a name for themselves the day they donned Invader disguises and snuck out to capture several Invader pupa. These were promptly devoured by the generals who then sent the gained information to decoders such as the talented Grimstalk who declared. "The enemy is illogical," at a local press conference. "The Invader destroys the host and kills itself in the process, chaos by any other name, is still chaos."

With this new understanding of the Invaders motivation, or lack of same, counter attacks were renewed with great fervor, and chemical disguises were attached. But, meanwhile, the host, Barney Templeton, continued to sicken prompting not a few Fidgets to fan their follicles furiously in an attempt to cool the overly heated child. A group of volunteers, Barney's Figeteers, spent hour after hour, singing uplifting songs while perched precariously on the tips of Barney's eardrums.

"This little host of mine, " they warbled, "shine, shine, shine, this little host of mine, we won't let you decline. This little host of mine, shine, shine, shine, let him shine, let him shine, let him shine."

But The Invader changed tactics and all of a sudden there were new enemies to contend with as it sent out waves of mutated troops. Like multi-legged zombies, they marched mindlessly, eating a path and leaving devastation in their wake.

Bottom-half held his side-mate closely as The Invader's shock troops swept over them, miraculously surviving the festering tide. Bottom-half chirped to the medics when being treated for burns, "they didn't recognize us! We must use this to our advantage!"

It seemed a coup, for the mutated troops did indeed fail to recognize the disguised Fidgets who, sounding the battle horn, went talon to talon to talon, dispatching the enemy with a fury. The host was their host, however small, and the tide was turned that day on what was to be called The Battle of Pancreas.

It was tricky, but it was done well, this battle, with many a Fidget losing its life while tickling for the white, mindless globs that came out of the host's infected organ. These globs were as apt to kill a Fidget as anything else, so it was a mighty gamble. But as the globs joined the effort, attacking The Invader alongside The Fidgets, it was deemed a success, and a monument was raised in honor of those who had died on the field.

Bottom-Half solemnly lay a wreath made from his rudimentary vertebra on the grave of his brave and beloved side-mate who had succumbed to her burns and had died in his arms. He cocked an eyestalk as the tinkling sounds of a child's laughter was heard shining through the clouds.

"Blmph," gurgled Sludge the Imp, snuggling and oozing in an attempt at comfort.

Bottom-Half held his Imp close to its side and smiled sadly through his tears.

Barney Templeton laughed again, his voice casting the scent of joy throughout the island and Bottom-half's smile grew a proud but weary node.

The price had been great but worth the cost. The war was over, and there was peace on the island with many a Fidget standing vigil.

"Blamph," Sludge the Imp blargled. "Blyth bah blag bah!"

DREE, ON WEDNESDAY

A GIRLISH VOICE ACCOMPANIED FROSTY WISPS of white breath. "Jack. Wake up." Jack woke up sniffing as a hound might, at the smell of toast.

"Jack." Impatiently now.

"I'm coming." called his twelve-year-old self. "I'm coming," whispered Jack. Twenty-three, years later, the voice still echoed. "Hurry, there's dragons!"

He would hurry, stumbling down the stairs, tripping into boots and trembling into a sweater. It was always like this on Wednesday and always would be.

Wednesday was when his cousin came to spend the day, and it didn't matter that Jack had received a D- on his math test, math did not exist on Wednesday.

Outside smells of autumn and spring mixed with butterscotch and scotch tape and frozen into Popsicles. There she was, just grinning and looking like a promise of Christmas day.

Jack had grinned back and knew in his twelve-year-old heart that he would love her forever. Forever was in a cave where Jack had kissed Dree for the very first time. It was in the cave that the two of them, as they would say to any that asked or even if they didn't, "Third cousins." swore with a blood shared and smeared that they would be together, forever.

Jack put on his shoes and stumbled down the stairs, and he can still hear her voice. "Hurry." And he does.

It was at the cave that Jack had given Dree a Valentine with the words "Be Mine Forever." It was in the cave that Dree had promised that she would be. Years into that forever, Jack walked - alone and lonely for she had died and left him with only her voice to follow.

Back to the cave where he had first touched her hair, the color of blood streaked mink and he did not go alone for Death followed nodding, and there she was, just grinning, smiling like the promise of Christmas day.

"Dree." He whispered.

"Forever," Dree whispered back. "Forever starts today."

AN ANKH FOR BECKY'S MOTHER

THE TATTOO WAS THAT OF a small ankh. Or, Becky grunted as she cut, it was supposed to look like one. Except it didn't, not really. It looked more like an eye with wings which would have been fine except that the wings were crooked.

Becky grunted again, slicing carefully with the razors sharp edge. The cut was the important thing. If she could have afforded to go to a tattoo parlor, she would have, but money, as always was tight. Doing the research, Becky had discovered the art of tattoo scarring, and it seemed simple enough, in theory anyway. You cut very thin lines, and when they healed, the designed skin would be raised slightly and became a pale white color.

It seemed doable.

Becky straightened, stretching, at the same time, holding a cloth to the ankle. Surprisingly, there was very little blood. Although, what little there was, was enough to make the outline of the eye with wings that might become an ankh, difficult to see. Becky grimaced as she pulled the cloth from where it clung to the matted, drying blood. The ankle was red and swollen around the slices.

Her mother lay in a hospital bed in a nursing home, her face set in a permanent scowl. Becky muttered to herself as she rolled a makeshift bandage around the leg and pulled on a clean, white, cotton sock. "There is time."

The next day, Becky, armed with home-made chicken soup, made her way along the usual route. It was a brisk walk to the station and two buses later; she was delivered to the front stoop of The Plaza Estates. Becky thought it was an annoying name. Wasn't a plaza the same as an estate? She didn't know, but she thought it was. It was all they could afford, regardless of the name.

Becky nodded to the taciturn receptionist who nodded back without any sign of recognition. This was not surprising, not many people recognized Becky even if they knew her. Born, Becky Lynn Butt, it was a name that practically guaranteed the solace of extra helpings of pudding. A growth surge at puberty had sent her soaring above her classmates, her red hair, as always, a curling mass that sat on the top of her head like a heap of coiled springs.

"Butt head! Butt-head Becky!" Those words had haunted her since grade school. Her pale, gray eyes, stared at her tormentors as she fingered a brownie, kept in her pocket to nibble on between classes. By eighth grade, she had weighed in at just shy of one hundred and seventy-five pounds and stood at 6'1. There had been no dates or school dances, no make-out sessions with anything but a pillow for Becky Lynn Butt.

And there had been no friends either, except for her mother.

"Don't mind those Cretans." Her mother would say as she baked, "It is not for all to be blessed with looks, besides, you have your health, and that is more important."

It was true, Becky did have her health. She was robust. That was her mother's word for it. But Becky's face did not reflect it, plagued with blackheads that competed with her freckles.

As she walked down the hallway of the nursing home, she did her best to ignore the smells of ammonia that persisted through the scent of the cabbage that The Plaza Estates seemed to serve on a daily basis. She carefully did not swing the bag containing the Tupperware container of chicken soup which was supposed to be checked in with the nurses. But, the nurses didn't care what Becky's mother ate. She could have been feeding her mother lye for all they seemed to care. Becky's mouth set itself in a grim line, her lipless mouth almost disappearing completely. Lye.

"Don't do that with your mouth, girl. It is so unattractive. You will never find a boyfriend with that mouth." Becky raised her chin but relaxed her lips as she strode toward her mother's room.

No, she thought to herself. No boyfriend for Becky.

She planted a smile on her freckled face and walked into her mother's room. Becky's mother had seemed to rally after her first stroke, but a series of small aftershocks had left her paralyzed down the one side and none too robust, her mother's word again, on the other. No matter how strong Becky was, her mother's needs went beyond her.

But, she reminded herself, not many mothers had daughters who visited daily. The Plaza Estates would have been far more horrific an ordeal had this not been the case. As she often did, Becky thought to herself, "Shoot me in the head, stick a gun up my nostrils and blow my brains out. Don't ever let this happen to me." But she smiled at her mother, who lay helplessly on her bed, smelling like urine.

Becky pulled the hospital chair over to the bed and placed the bag with the chicken soup carefully on the small metal dresser, beside the small framed picture brought from home. Flowers. She sighed as she sat down and then noticed, with annoyance, that the white sock was stained a brownish red.

"Good morning," Becky said in a forced and cheerful sounding voice. "I brought some soup." She avoided looking at her mother's face. She could feel that eye, hooded in flaps of aging layers of paper-thin skin staring at her. "Let's get you cleaned up first."

The Plaza Estates was not great on hygiene.

Becky patted her mother and then, from the small, adjoining bathroom, prepared a basin of warm water, soap, and a washcloth. Carefully and thoroughly, she cleaned her mother's body and replaced the wetted diaper with a dry one. "Up through the nose, into the brain, splatter it against a wall. I don't care. Don't ever let this happen to me," Becky muttered as she pulled on the plastic tab to hold the diaper in place. "Up through the nose." She darted a quick look at her mother, whose one eye seemed to blaze. So. She was aware today which was not always a good thing, even if one would think it should be.

She gripped her mother's leg. "Hey there. Nice and clean. Hungry?"

Her mother's eye stared back, and from the one side of her mouth came a sound, "Ughnn nuuh."

Which really could have meant anything.

After pressing the button on the bed to raise the upper half, Becky carefully spooned soup into her mother's mouth. You had to press down hard on that button. The mattress was far from new and smelled as if it had been left in an ally to rot. For all Becky knew, it had been. "Good. Good soup," Becky said, as she wiped her mother's face with a small towel. "It is not as good as the soup you used to make, but not bad, not bad."

Her mother's eye slowly blinked.

"How is Ian?" Becky forced the lie. "He is doing great in med school. This is what he gave me for, I guess …" Becky stumbled a bit on the story. "For, well, two years in med school. It's a lot. Look. Isn't it pretty?" She held out the chain of the necklace she had bought for herself.

"You can't look me in the face when you tell those lies," her mother had said, and it was true. "I can always tell when you are lying."

But Becky looked into her mother's face, unflinching, as she continued, "I wish, and he wishes too, that he could, you know, visit." Becky stood up and reached for the basin, the dirty washcloth floating in the soiled water. "They don't allow it. This place." She looked at her mother directly. "They have rules."

Becky rinsed the basin and refilled it with clean water. She grabbed another cloth. It wouldn't do to let the tattoo become infected. Sitting down, she took off the stained sock, then carefully unwrapped the dried bandage revealing her handiwork. Becky's small eyes widened. Why the tattoo didn't look like anything at all!

"What? It. It looks ..." Becky's thin mouth closed with a snap.

Along the one side where the ankh shape was supposed to be, only one side was raised, and even that, choppily. The wings, well, they did sort of look like wings, but the eye was nothing but a clotted hole and failed to resemble its intention.

"In another time, there would be priests. You know? Like Egyptian priests? And there would be incense and stuff." Becky swallowed, greatly disappointed in her failed attempt. Her mother breathed, the long raspy sounds of a mammal drowning in its phlegm. Sometimes, Becky imagined that she could hear her mother's moist lungs, pink and gray. "And cats," She blurted. "Your organs would go into magic jars with symbols on them." She sniffed. "Well then. We do what we can. That is what you taught me."

She left the eye in the tattoo alone. Better to let it heal and start again or the whole thing would have a great big dot in it, and it would look just wrong, wrong, wrong. The wings could be left alone but what the ankh needed, besides having the edges edgier, was a tail. Yes. Never mind about it being a winged eye. The wings could stay. No matter that it looked, if you really looked, like an eye with wings. Why settle? She had started with the idea of cutting the shape of an ankh, and that was what she was going to do.

"Yep." Becky murmured as she cut around the shape

of what was to be a real ankh, one that looked like an ankh. There would be no misunderstanding. None of any kind. "Yep," Becky repeated. "This is going to look right. Egyptian."

The straight edged razor slipped on the curve of the outer circle, and Becky cursed under her breath, then shot a look of apology at her mother. They did not swear. There were other words. Becky gripped the edge of the razor and cut inward, she would have to widen that outer edge of the circle, and if she had to dig out little pieces of flesh, well, you had to do what you had to do, and that was that.

The razor slipped, cutting Becky's thumb. "I need a new one or something." She mumbled around the thumb in her mouth, "And I need to cut deeper on each side. Well," she sighed, "it's getting late, and it's almost meds time." Becky cleared her throat looking into her mother's aware eye, the one that looked at her daughter and said, what? What was her mother trying to say?

Becky patted her mother as she tidied up. She drew up the sheet and the covers that she had brought from home. "You will sleep soon. Dream a happy dream, as you always used to say."

Back home, the same route, only backward, she walked into the house that she used to share with her mother. "A timeshare," Her mother used to quip. Becky had never really known what her mother had meant by that, but her mother had a lot of sayings. Becky had listened often enough; her thick thighs gripped the edge of the kitchen stool as her mother gave her recipes to sort.

Becky's mother had often tried to teach her daughter to cook, urging her daughter to eat, eat, eat. There were moments where, later, when Becky put her fingers down her throat, having eaten far more than anyone should. But Becky did not like to vomit. No Bulimia for Becky.

She walked through the small, silent house looking at her mother's unused bedroom with its closed door. The plants Becky forgot about sat dying in their corners. "Ian. I'm home." She called out. It was a joke but even so.

"I'm lonely," Becky told the room as she fondled her uninspiring chest. But then she smacked herself on the knee. "Stop it," she told herself. "Stop it." She walked over to the small kitchen and opened a cabinet, taking out the box of razor blades, putting them into her purse before she forgot.

The next morning, Becky, armed with overcooked porridge, set herself onto the familiar route and arrived at the usual destination. It was the same receptionist as yesterday. Again, she didn't seem to recognize Becky. "Or," Becky thought. "Or, she does recognize me, but I don't matter, and that is probably what it is."

Becky took a deep breath and walked down the hall; she would try to hold that one breath until she got to her mother's room and could open a window. But she could only hold her breath for so long, and it always seemed to give out right after she passed the dining room. She exhaled deeply, wrinkled her nose and continued walking.

In her mother's room, the sheets were soiled. "If this

were Egypt," Becky told her mother. "We would, you know, put your brain into a jar. I would keep that jar on a shelf. If this were Egypt."

Becky uncovered the tattoo and gave a small wail of dismay. Her eyes met those of her mother's, whose eyes communicated, what? What was she trying to say? "I don't know," Becky cried. "I don't know why it doesn't look right. And it looks all sore, and I didn't bring anything." She looked at the oozing redness of the lower calf. "It's infected. Damn. Damn!" Becky swore. "Yes, I know that it is a bad word!" She got up and walked to the bathroom. "I'll clean it as best as I can because that is all I can do right now." She looked at her mother who stared at her with her one eye. "What?" Becky demanded, "What are you trying to tell me?"

Becky closed her eyes thinking and then, "Oh. Of course. They would have something like that here. And nobody ever notices me. You are right, mother. You are always right." Becky smiled. "I am going on a mission."

Becky snuck down the hallway of The Plaza Estates although, she knew she didn't have to. Nobody was going to see her. It would have been far more unusual at that time of day for there to be any staff around at all. The few residents who could still hobble out of bed, stood at their respective doorways like refugees, haunted and withered. Once, maybe twice, Becky had seen a light in the eyes of one of the ghosts, as she called them. But whether it had been for hope for conversation, or hope for something else, it was difficult to determine.

There was a spring in her step as she stalked the

corridors, searching different rooms. Mother was always right. Stuff like that had to be somewhere in a place like this. Becky searched the lounges, but it was only when she came to the inner hallway, that she found the supply room.

Becky tiptoed into the room. There it was. The blade glistened. Its stainless steel handle positively glittered. She gazed around in rapture and almost gasped at the sight of it all. There were gauze bandages. There were ointment and hand sanitizer and cotton balls in jars.

Jars. Like in Egypt - except made of glass but that was okay. That was more than okay.

It was meant to be. It was a gift, yes, a blessing. There were sacks, laundry sacks she assumed, and Becky joyfully filled them with necessities. She was extra mindful with the stainless steel blade, saving it for last, wrapping it into a handy washcloth.

Sneaking down the empty corridor toward her mother's room, Becky almost missed the flowers. They stood on a counter just outside of the outer circle where she had found the door to the supply room. It was stealing, but that didn't matter. She giggled like a child as she stuffed the arrangement into her sack.

Her mother loved flowers, and her eye watched as Becky arranged them on the table.

"The dead were revered in Egypt," Becky said, taking her supplies out of the bag and placing them on her mother's bed. "Oh, I know you are not dead yet, I know that." She patted her mother's leg comfortingly, ignoring that eye that seemed to widen as Becky pulled down her sock.

"I know you have never liked tattoos," Becky said, as she cut with the scalpel, biting her lip with concentration, the blade was very sharp, and it wouldn't do, no, it wouldn't do at all, to cut too deeply. "Mine is just for practice. Don't worry, by the time I get to do yours; I will have it down pat."

She stared into her mother's glaring eye. "Practice makes perfect, isn't that what you always say? Said?"

Becky cut. Blood dripped to the floor until later when, nodding in satisfaction, she gently pulled the covers up to expose her mother's thin, pale legs and only then did Becky's mother make a sound, a grunt. "Nuh, guh!"

"What was that?" Becky looked into her mother's drooping face. "Oh. It will be an ankh. Like, from Egypt. See?" She stood up and lifted her leg for her mother to view. "Like mine." Her mother grunted again as Becky cleaned off the edge of the scalpel on the edge of the bed and began to cut deeply. "I know mine is messy, but yours, I promise you, yours will be perfect." She swallowed audibly. "I love you, mom."

BARTHOLOMEW AND THE BURGLAR

"Dag nab it!" exclaimed Bartholomew. He slowly eased his aching body from his bed, slid his feet into slippers and creakily walked toward the bathroom to relieve his bladder. Old age had its disadvantages, and repeated trips to the bathroom were only one of many. This would be his fourth trip tonight.

He muttered and swore as he stood in front of the toilet, finally seating himself upon his porcelain throne in exasperation. Bartholomew's bladder had sent **its** urgent message to his brain but had failed to inform a certain another part of his body. So he sat fuming as he waited, and that is when he heard the noise.

It was an unusual noise. Bartholomew cocked his head as he listened. His hearing was in good order at least, and he was accustomed to noises: the creaks the house made as it settled, and the rattle of a certain window in response to large trucks—he knew them all. But this, this noise was not one of those.

Bartholomew pulled his boxer shorts up over his scrawny flanks, walked slowly over to the bathroom window and peered into the darkness. But there was nothing to be seen. He started to turn when he heard the noise again. It was a scratching sound, and it sounded as if it was coming from the back porch.

"Raccoons?" he pondered, muttering as he tottered quickly toward the stairs. If it was raccoons, he had a nice surprise for them: a shotgun he kept hidden in the closet by the front door.

With one age-spotted hand on the banister, Bartholomew crept carefully down the stairs, his bladder complaining the entire time. "Dang it," he cussed and groped himself through his boxers, giving himself a squeeze and a bit of a shake.

Through the living room and into the kitchen he toddled, bladder aching. He reached for a large flashlight that hung beside the fire extinguisher on the wall, walked around the corner that led to the porch, switched on the flashlight and aimed its bright beam on the sliding glass doors.

It is difficult to say who was the most surprised, Bartholomew, or the man that the bright light revealed.

"Ah!" screamed Bartholomew.

The man screamed as well as he backed away from the light, staggering out of view.

Bartholomew stumbled back through the kitchen and living room gasping, "A burglar, oh my gosh and goodness!" Flinging back the closet door, he grabbed his shotgun and then scurried back to the sliding glass doors which he fumbled to open, almost spitting to himself in disgust as he felt a few trickles of urine drip down his trembling leg.

But the burglar was gone.

Bartholomew pointed the flashlight here and there and then carefully slid open the porch door. Hugging the gun close to his side, he ventured onto the wooden porch, shining the light across the backyard. The cuff of a pant leg came into view. The leg did not move, and Bartholomew tiptoed stealthily across the porch to the top of the stairs and then looked down.

The man lay unmoving, hands above his head on the

flagstone, apparently dead. Bartholomew gave a small moan and, gun under his arm, fearfully walked down the stairs, shining the flashlight onto the dead man's face.

The man sat up suddenly, and Bartholomew shrieked in surprise. Clutching at his chest, he retreated a few paces and fell backward, striking his head on the bottom of the porch stairs.

The burglar lurched to his feet, "Wha' are you doin' here?" slurred the burglar. "Wha' are you doin' in my *house?*"

Bartholomew grabbed for the shotgun and shot wildly, striking many innocent hedges, then, clutching his chest once more, fell to his side and gasped, "Heart!"

The burglar lurched to Bartholomew's side, reaching for Bartholomew's wrist, perhaps to take his pulse, we will never know, for that was when Bartholomew shot the man in the face.

"Ha! I fooled you good now, didn't I?" Bartholomew screamed as he clutched at his chest for real, falling on top of the drunken man who had wandered into his yard. Bartholomew gave a last shout of triumph, either for defending his home or finally emptying his bladder or both.

A BIRD IN HAND

ONCE UPON A TIME, IN a small secluded forest, The Fairy Mab tucked in her three visiting grandchildren, Iolanthe, Arafel and Emmaleth, having ensconced them upon a lovely, swaying tulip.

"Tell us a bedtime story, Grandma?" little Iolanthe pleaded, eye's large and beseeching.

Arefel bounced in excited agreement, while Emmaleth fluttered tiny, translucent baby fairy wings and lisped, *"Yeth, pleath?"*

Mab smiled at her beloved grandchildren and perched on a nearby leaf, and began her tale.

"There once was a mortal woman named Jean who was married and didn't like it. Her husband, Merv, was neither attractive nor intelligent, but Jean had turned thirty-five, and her mother had turned desperate."

"What ith desperth?" Emmaleth asked.

"Shh," said Iolanthe.

Merv was a steady worker, at times, and he belched appreciatively after every meal.

Mab gave a delicate belch and her grandbabies giggled.

"Now, this mortal man did not take his wife to nice restaurants, but he did take her bowling regularly. Jean supposed she should be grateful, but she wasn't. No, she was not. She sat at her kitchen table one day, and she began to weep in great despair.

"Becausth thee was thad," nodded Emmaleth.

Mab leaned over and tweaked her youngest grandchild's soft, infant's cheek. *"She was, she was very sad,"* Grandma Mab agreed, *"but just then..."*

A small bird peered in through the open window with his wee head tilted on one side. Mab cocked her head to one side, sparkling as she did, and the three baby fairies all tilted their heads with her.

Jean looked up greatly startled as the bird began to speak.

"People!" The bird grumbled, "day and night; whine, whine, whine!"

"I've gone crazy," Jean whimpered and began to cry.

"Why was she crying?" Arafel asked her grandmother.

"Well you see, " Mab replied as she smoothed the golden hair from little Arafel's forehead, *"mortals do not really believe in talking birds."*

"That's thilly," Emmaleth declared stoutly. Her older sister Iolanthe nodded in agreement as she snuggled into the tulip, causing it to sway gently back and forth.

"Yes well…mortals," Mab said vaguely. *"You will understand when you are older."*

The bird snorted.

"You *can* talk!" said Jean.

"I think, therefore I am," the bird snarled. "What else would you like, the theory of relativity?"

"What is the theory of, um…levaty?" asked a confused Iolanthe who was shushed by Arafel.

Mab cleared her throat.

Jean watched wide-eyed as the dainty, scowling bird paced the length of her windowsill, muttering darkly. After some time had passed, she tentatively asked, "Having a bad day?"

"Madam," said the bird, "I will have you know," and he puffed up his chest feathers, "I am a Sparrow!"

Mab stuck out her chest and made a serious face, flapping her arms as she did. The little girls giggled and the tiny bells of laughter caused a series of twinkle lights to appear upon their tulip bed for a brief period as if touched by a ray of moonlight. Mab nodded approvingly.

"Okay," said Jean. "Got it. Birds are talking to me. Yup. Nothing crazy here!"

"She still doesn't believe that birds can talk," whispered Arefel to her youngest sister who nodded as she stuck the end of her braid into her mouth and sucked on it. Mab removed it with an admonishing finger.

"I suppose you don't bother reading fairy tales?" sneered the Sparrow sarcastically.

"Not really," Jean responded.

The three little fairies all gasped. *"She doesn't read fairy tales?"* cried Iolanthe in disbelief. Little Emmaleth's eyes grew round, and she gasped, *"Whaths wrong with her?"*

"She's dumb."

"We are Sparrows, and we have a motto," Mab continued in a louder voice.

Arefel piped, *"Will you do the voice? Please?"*

"Yeth pleath!" begged Emmaleth, almost bouncing off of the Tulip. *"Pleath do a thparrow voicth!"*

Mab began again and sort of twittered as she said, "We Sparrows have a motto. Proudly to the aid of women in distress."

"What's a motto?" Arafel asked.

"I'm hungry," said Iolanthe.

"I'm thirsty!" said Emmaleth.

Mab looked at her grandchildren in silence, and then, with a flick of her wings, flew to a nearby bush where she gathered some berries.

"Thees mad," Emmaleth lisped.

"Shh," whispered Iolanthe.

"Well, thee is."

"How can you tell?"

"Listen!" Arafel nodded. *"Emmy is right."*

"Ish not noishee!"

And it wasn't, the forest had become a silent place, where no frog dared to croak nor bee to buzz.

Mab distributed the berries equally and continued her tale as he grandchildren nibbled, berry juice staining their faces and hands and dribbling onto their clean frocks. Mab said nothing but sighed as she snatched at a leaf and cleaned their faces.

"The bird cocked his head thoughtfully."

Mab cocked her head and tried to look like a Sparrow.

"Mind you; it used to be damsels. Come to think of it," the bird added, "it used to be maidens."

Mab chuckled to herself, and Iolanthe immediately asked, *"What's so funny, grandma?"*

To which Mab quickly collected herself, recalling how young her grandchildren were, but it was too late.

"What's a Damsel?" asked Iolanthe.

"Whatch a damshel?"

"Never mind," Mab quickly replied and returned to the story.

"Um…?" inquired Jean, who didn't know either.

"Thee didn't know what a damsthel wasth?" lisped Emmaleth.

Mab sighed.

"We had to change with the times," said the bird.

"I see," marveled Jean.

"You still don't get it, do you?" hissed the bird.

"I don't get it either," admitted Arefel.

"That's cuz you are thtupid," said Emmaleth.

"I am here to rescue you!" the Sparrow roared.

Mab gave a mighty roar which temporarily earned her a moment's respite. Even the frogs in the nearby area fell quiet.

Jean stared at the bird, and the bird angrily stared back at her, and then, he shook his tiny head in disgust.

"Did thee sthmell bad?" asked Emmaleth, greatly confused, and her two sisters sniggled.

Mab stared down at her precious grandchildren.

"Jean did not want to aggravate the Sparrow further," Mab said sternly."

The three little fairies looked back at her and then at each other and had the grace to stay silent. Emmaleth's braid had found its way back into her rosebud mouth, but this time, Mab did not remove it. Emmaleth often chewed on her braid before she slept. Maybe she would sleep.

"What can you do? Do you have powers?" the mortal woman asked the bird.

"So," Iolanthe asked curiously, *"Jean believes birds can talk now?"*

Mab heaved a small sigh and leaned over, giving Iolanthe a pat. *"Yes, she now believes that birds can talk."* Mab looked down at the three young fairies, and they innocently stared back. There was a moment of blessed quiet.

"I can..." the bird's feathers deflated with its bravado, and it began to look uncertain.

"What's bravado mean?" asked Iolanthe.

"Girls," Mab sighed. *"Do you want to hear the story or not?"*

"I do!" Arefel said quickly.

Emmaleth grunted adorably as she drooled on her braid, *"Me thood!"*

"This is my first time," the Sparrow *eventually* offered as it clicked his beak with a snap.

Mab clapped her hands, and the little fairies squealed.

"I can give you some advice!" said the Sparrow.

"Well, that's always good! What advice can you give me? Jean eagerly asked.

The Sparrow warbled and began to ruffle his feathers.

Mab gave a nice impression of a warble and lifted her arms as if they were wings, but Emmaleth interrupted her grandmother's imitation ruffle.

"The sptharrow sounds pithed."

Mab gasped. *"Miss Emmaleth Asrai Acacia Fae! Where did you learn that word?"*

Arefel pinched her youngest sister who smacked her back with one tiny wing.

"Thopt it!"

"You started it!"

Iolanthe scolded, *"Both of you stop acting like Mumiai, or we won't hear the rest of the story!"*

Mab looked at her grandchildren, first one and then the second, and then to Emmaleth, who pouted around her braid.

"We Sparrows have given advice to the famous!" said Mab, sounding like herself and not the slightest bit like a Sparrow.

"For example?" countered Jean.

"What about Cinderella?" demanded the Sparrow.

"What *about* Cinderella?" retorted Jean.

"We directed Prince Charming to the step meanie's house," reported the Sparrow smugly.

"Seriously!" said Mab as she leaned over and put a halting hand on a wiggling Emmaleth, who was being punched by Arafel, who was being pinched by Iolanthe.

"Oh!" breathed the outraged bird, "I forgot that little miss "Sparrows wear army boots" over here doesn't read her fairy tales! I will have you know," he yelled, "without us, Cindy would never have become a princess. I mean she is *fat* now, but she is *royal!"*

"I am sorry," Jean apologized. "Please advise me, great Sparrow?"

Emmaleth continued to wiggle, and Iolanthe stuck one wing up.

"Yes?" Mab snapped tiredly.

"I think that Emmy needs to use the toadstool."

Mab hurriedly scooped up the smallest fairy and flew her quickly to a nearby patch of fungus.

"She is getting mad, you can tell," Iolanthe said to

her sister. *"The two of you better stop, or she is going to turn you both into ugly bats."*

"She will not; grandma loves us," Arafel responded tearfully. *"She would never turn us into bats!"*

"Yep," Iolanthe said. *"Ugly, smelly little bats."*

"She will not!"

"Will too!"

"Will not!"

Will too!"

Mab flew back with Emmaleth, forcibly unhooked her granddaughter's sweet smelling arms that were gripping her around the neck as if they were strangling vines. She placed the little fairy between the two arguing sisters, and scolded, *"I want the two of you to stop acting like Ekimmu, right this second!"*

"She started it!" Arafel sobbed.

"Did not!" hollered Iolanthe.

Little Emmaleth's bottom lip quivered, and she began to whimper.

"Iolanthe said you would turn us into bats!"

Emmaleth began to howl—even though she liked bats and wouldn't have minded being turned into one.

Mab quickly scooped Emmaleth back into her arms and rocked her." *I would never turn you into a bat."*

"But -but I want to be thurned into a bat!" wailed Emmaleth.

Mab rocked her a little bit faster and gave the other two little fairies in the tulip her sternest look as she patted Emmelth on the back.

"Ahem," Mab said.

The Sparrow stuck his beak up in the air and tapped the windowsill with one claw.

"Please, oh please give me some advice?" Jean asked desperately.

The Sparrow sighed with importance and not a little impatience, "Easy!" he said. "Just leave!"

"Leave?" Jean echoed blankly.

"Elementary," said the Sparrow smugly.

"Leave?" Jean all but shrieked, "That's all I get?"

The Sparrow pulled his shoulders above his head and gave its finest and best beady glare.

Mab glared at her wriggling grandbabies.

"Leave," chuckled Jean. "Now, why didn't I think of that!"

Iolanthe opened her mouth but quickly closed it again as her grandmother gave her a fierce look. Mab rocked for a moment of quiet with the only sound coming from Emmaleth who, on her grandmother's lap, moistly chewed on her braid.

The Sparrow fluffed his feathers again, and Jean quickly said, "Oh bird, I'm not trying to insult you. That is very good advice, but I haven't any place to leave *to!* And," she explained, "while Sparrows may not need money, people do."

"*Wuffs mummy?*" said Emmaleth indistinctly, her braid slipping out of her mouth as she did but Mab chose to ignore the question and stuffed the braid back into Emmaleth's mouth.

"Money," the horrified Sparrow whispered hoarsely. "I forgot about money!"

"That's understandable," Jean said, trying to comfort the distraught and suddenly trembling bird, "you being a Sparrow and all."

"That's no excuse!" The bird waved his wings, flapping in distress. "I should have thought about that. Mortals need money! It's written right there in The Sparrow's Handbook.I have failed my first mission!"

"Well," soothed Jean, "I am sure your boss will understand."

"No she won't!" the panicked bird wailed. "You don't know her! She is a troll and besides, we sparrows have a one hundred percent success rate!"

Jean whistled, "One hundred percent?"

"Yeah," sighed the Sparrow sadly.

"Don't take it so hard," said Jean. "Here, have a crust."

"How can you think of food at a time like this?" screamed the Sparrow.

"What if I gave you a letter of recommendation?" offered Jean. "Would that help?"

"No," muttered the despondent avian, "but that's awfully nice of you."

"Don't mention it," grinned Jean.

The Sparrow flew to the kitchen table and paced, deep in thought, taking a sip of Jean's coffee. "Money," he mused. "I do have a friend who is a goldsmith of sorts."

"Really? A Goldsmith?" responded Jean politely.

"That's it!" screeched the Sparrow, hopping up and down in excitement. "It's not exactly by the book but," the Sparrow twittered, all smiling beak, "you could sleep on the couch, do the dishes maybe? What do you say?"

"I don't know," Jean answered doubtfully.

"Do you know how to spin?"

"Huh? Spin what?"

"Oh, never mind! Grubs! I can't just leave you here!"

"One hundred percent, you said?" questioned Jean.

"Chirp!"

"Okay," Jean decided, "maybe wishes do come true. Hey! What's the matter?"

"Oh, don't mind me," sobbed the Sparrow, "I always cry at happy endings."

"That Jean really flipped," said another mortal named Mabel to her best friend Sally, "I heard she left her husband, and she took nothing but birdseed with her."

"I know," giggled Sally, "and three suitcases of straw!"

"*I know where she went!*" Iolanthe squealed.

"*Me too!*" Arefel squeaked.

"*Thee wenth to….*"

"*Rumple….*"

"*Don't say it,*" warned Mab. "*Don't ever say that name!*" With that, Mab finished tucking her three grandchildren in, sang until they were asleep, and then went for a much-needed cup of nectar.

THE DAY THAT MANY THINGS HAPPENED

(No collection would be complete without a representation from my series, Vampire Therapy. This is one of many stories that comprise, Vampire Therapy, The Chronicles of The Cat's Ass Boutique. S.)

PETRA AND DUKE SPRAWLED NAKED and entwined on a stack of bean bags that lay squished together on the darkened dance floor of The Cats's Ass Boutique. It wasn't a sex thing. Duke would have been more than willing but the difference in their ages counted, because no matter what Petra may have wished for otherwise, Duke would always be a child to her.

Petra took comfort in Duke. The feel of his bare skin, freshly warmed, was like no other feeling and after so many years, nudity had simply stopped being an issue.

Plus, it was time for a bedtime story. Mr Abraham didn't mind. His minions could do as they liked with one another. Well, Duke and Petra could... Shebat, on the other hand, Mr. Abraham's run off minion/wife could not. Would not, if Mr. A could find her, which he couldn't, although that did not stop him from trying.

The staff of The Cat's Ass Boutique never forgot this although they did their best to ignore it. This and the fact that the very Fates themselves seemed to take an interest in them (and wasn't that odd!), popping in and handing out "Special kittens," and Duke's amulet and not a single one of the Vampires knew what any of it meant. Why were the kittens "Special?" What was up with the amulet? What was going on?

It was disturbing.

And then, the whole Leprechaun thing.. although Lilly did seem to be feeling better and had taken to wearing "Message" tee shirts with slogans ranging from the positive, "I Heart Death Metal," to the philosophical, "If history repeats itself, could we have dinosaurs?"

Nobody minded now that Lilly had stopped crying, there were very few rodents left in the neighborhood, but the poor girl had been positively anemic and what with Mr. Abraham's limitations on feeding, rounding up rodents had been the best that Duke and Petra could do at the time.

Petra ran her fingers over Duke's smooth, warm back, and inhaled his scent. She moved a slim foot against his shin and he shivered and held her close. There was so much stress around them and there was comfort in the cuddle and so they squeezed against each other, getting comfortable.

Petra cleared her throat.

"It was a beautiful summer day in the town of Temagazombie, on the day that Selma Mae Cross got married in the backyard that belonged to her mother's first ex- husband, Lester Smutten.

"Who is Lester Smutten...? I forget," murmured a sleepy Duke. He had settled into a sprawl with his muscular arms behind his head, with Petra, her tousled head of red tinted curls draped across his strong bare shoulder.

"Lester Smutten was Patricia's first husband and he was not the bride's father. Selma Mae, the blushing

bride to be, was the product of Lester's ex wife's second marriage to a man named Diego."

Duke blinked.

"Diego was Patricia's second ex-husband and they had a daughter and she was getting married in her Mother's FIRST husband's backyard."

Duke blinked again.

"Selma Mae was getting married in the backyard of the ex husband of her mother's SECOND husband, the one who WASN'T her father," offered Petra hopefully and Duke frowned. Petra sighed.

"Selma Mae's mother, Patricia, divorced Selma's Mae's father, Diego, and then married her third and current spouse, Jane Goodey."

"Sooo...,Duke ventured slowly, "Patrica was married to Lester but they didn't have any kids?"

"That's right, Duke."

"...And Lester got a divorce from Patricia?"

"Yes, she did," smiled Petra.

"Then she married Diego and they had a kid?"

"That's right, Dukey," Petra reached over and tucked an errant lock of Duke's wheat colored hair behind his ear. "... and then Patricia divorced HIM and married Jane."

"Okay," Duke yawned.

"That was not what had the townspeople tongues wagging...

And it wasn't because Selma Mae was getting married to her long term girlfriend, Rebecca, either. This was *interesting*, true, but what people pondered most furiously was why on earth was Selma Mae and Rebecca exchanging vows in the backyard of Patricia's first husband, Lester. Why him?

"Why not him?" Duke opened one eye and peered at Petra who chucked him under the chin and continued,

"To many of the women, and a great number of the men of Temagazombie, the pervading question remained, why was Lester Smutten, (of all people)...that modest mouse of a man..., that frumpy, short, skinny, unassuming sot of a man..."

Duke snickered.

"Why was Lester having the best summer party of the decade, a lesbian wedding in HIS backyard and how was he getting away with it?

Petra sat up enough to hold up her fingers in air italics and Duke snatched the petite red head back to him as if she were a teddy bear.

"Everyone in the town either knew or had heard of Lester's second wife, the terrifying Veronica."

"Was she a monster?" asked Duke.

"Worse than that, Dukey, she was a bitch," replied Petra.

"Veronica had not been seen for days... and it is true, many did not miss her but it was just plain ODD that Lester's first wife, Patrica and her wife Jane, had set up camp at Lester's. Why was that?

"Hmm," Duke hummed, half asleep.

"It remained unanswered, and like an annoying splinter, it festered it's way to the surface of many a conversation!"

"*You are better than a television show,*" *Duke kissed the top of Petra's head and she smiled.*

"*Had Veronica left Lester...?*" *Petra continued the story,*

If Veronica has left Lester, why didn't her few friends know about it and was it because of Patricia? Was boring Lester Smutten back with his lesbian ex-wife? And what about Patricia's wife, Jane? Just what in hell was going on?

Duke rolled over onto his stomach and Petra sat up, smoothing her hand down Duke's back with her fingertips making Duke purr in contentment.

Cat, Petra's "special kitten" also purred and Lilly's "special kitten", whatever she was naming it this week, wrestled nearby. By the sound of the rustling they made, the "special Kittens" had found some leftover confetti from the party of the night before.

Parties were always exhausting for Duke. As a bartender extraordinaire, he didn't so much as mix drinks as he did magic while creating them to the awe and adulation of the regulars of The Cat's Ass Boutique.

"Lester Smutton was enjoying his notoriety and on the day of the wedding, he dressed with rare attention to detail. Selma Mae's mother, Patricia had asked him permission if she could use his backyard for the nuptials and he had said yes, not because she was a lesbian, which was rather exciting news, or even that Selma's daughter and fiancee were lesbian's, which was, and he had to agree with the majority on this, very interesting, but he had said "yes" because his wife, his second wife... Veronica had said, "No."

In fact, she had denied permission so vehemently that as she spat out the word, her lower denture plate had flown out of her mouth and hit Lester on the chin.

Duke snickered again.

"Veronica, with hands on ample thighs… that had never parted for either childbirth or passion, had cawed her disapproval and with an unusual amount of spittle and sibilance continued with a grand torrent of objection, "No! I said no! I meant no, I mean, no!" and as Veronica bent down to pick up her forcefully ejected denture from where it lay on the rose-printed braided rug, she bumped her head against Lester's balding pate as he stooped to retrieve it for her, prepared to offer an apology and to acquiesce to his wife's decision.

Something changed in Lester at that very moment…." *said Petra and she tickled Cat, who had wandered over to listen.*

Veronica had picked the wrong day to refuse. Lester, wincing and rubbing the back of his balding, round head found himself saying, "Oh yes it will! There will be a wedding in MY backyard for the daughter of MY first wife and that is final!"

Lester hadn't heard from Veronica since and then it all just became rather complicated what with everyone and their questions and it was just easier to shrug helplessly and look mysterious. He had tried calling Veronica at her sister's house, he had even left a message. Really, what else could one do? Lester was sure that his wife was *somewhere* but in the meantime, he, Lester Smutton was the proud host of a backyard lesbian wedding and he hoped his wife wouldn't return soon enough to ruin it!

He had never been this popular.

Petra stopped talking, thinking Duke had gone to sleep.

"What happened then, Petra?" asked Duke plaintively, cupid's bow of a mouth in a slight pout.

"Well, the wedding was an ample affair," said Petra, with over fifty guests invited and more who would surely stop in with a bottle of wine and a camera. Veronica Smutten's garden backed out onto the vista of Bright River, it was a lovely spot for a wedding. It was perhaps fortunate that Veronica herself would not be in attendance... although not so fortunate for Veronica... considering what happened next.

Selma Mae was later to have remarked, "It's funny how the dykes all went kablooehy the day of the wedding. Get it? Dykes?" and you really had to hand it to her for being a good sport about it all but really, it hadn't been all that funny when the locks of the dams that held Temagazombie's flowing Bright River reset themselves to zero and no one at the reservoir noticed that a switch that should have been turned on, wasn't.

The rented, trained doves that were to be released after the vows had given no warning of impending doom. Tanya, the coat check girl was to remark on that. "Birds," she was to say, later, "You know? You would think?" but that was afterward. That day, that Sunday, the day of the wedding and so many other things, Lester, playing his role as "provider of the backyard", sat smugly in his garden chair. There was no man in Temagazombie that could beat Lester for having a better party story. An outdoor lesbian wedding party easily beat out Thomas Baily's, "The Stripper Who Slipped." Heck, he Lester Smutton wouldn't even have to exaggerate. He had witnesses!

It had all been going so well...

Selma Mae's wedding dress did not steal the show that day, which was sad but then, she had never been much of a looker, but the other bride, Rebecca, with her raven black hair, her brilliant blue eyes and a plunging neckline did.

"Mmhm," agreed Duke.

Lester didn't notice the tug on his sleeve by his next chair neighbor, Ernest Tophandle. Ernest had been fidgeting throughout the entire pre-affair, twitching with envy, thinking to himself, *"This could have been my backyard. Why couldn't my daughter be a lesbian? Why is the wedding in Lester's backyard. Selma Mae isn't Lester's daughter! Where the hell is Veronica?"*

Tanya, the coat check girl, that winsome young thing, whose cheerful freckled face positively seemed to beam with youthful vigor, wondered this herself but when the wave that preceded the flood hit Lester's floating dock, sending barrels crashing against against each other and causing trees to groan, wherever Veronica was or wasn't suddenly became a moot point.

It all started with a roaring sound. The guests were seated in rented wicker chairs that formed a semi circle around a free standing, white painted, wooden arch.

The many guests of the bride and the other bride cocked their heads in unison, looking not at Rebecca, who stood waiting, but beyond her to wherever the sound was coming from.

"Construction?" Dermot Selmpy guessed, but then Patricia, seated as was proper, in the front row next to Jane, shouted in alarm! She stood up and pointed as a great wash of tumbling wooden lawn furniture, trees and other debris came charging toward Lester's beloved dock as if Poseidon himself had risen from the bottom of Bright River hell bent on destruction.

"Noooo..! shouted an angered Lester and whether it was because of the doomed dock or the poor timing of the flood, it was hard to say. As the guests either ran screaming or stood watching, depending on their temperament, poor, plain, outshone and now disaster struck Selma Mae, stood braying tears at the top of the porch, never having managed to walk carefully down the steps to the tune of the wedding march. It was clear that the party was over.

"Poor Selma Mae," murmured Duke.

Mabel Chesternut was a decent woman, treasurer of The Very Busy Bees and co organizer of the bimonthly rummage sale, held that very day. "La!" she said as she looked at the unexpected knife sticking out of her chest.

It could be said later that it was a bit of positive news that the flood had not reached Mabel's house and thus caused no damage but even had Mabel known of this, she would not have appreciated the fact being far too busy surviving at the time.

Duke squirmed into the bean bag and rolled once more onto his back. Petra rested her head on his stomach, Cat, her "special kitten" snuggled into the crook of her knee.

Darren Goodwitch, a young man with an old past...

"I LIKE that!" Duke grinned at Petra, "that sounded like a line from a movie!"

"I try," Petra grinned up at him and Cat showed his tiny fangs in a yawn.

Darren Goodwitch was part of the crew that worked on Mabel's roof, and a really nice job they had done..., he had watched from above as, through the sliding door window, Mabel could be seen carrying the tin cash box she had brought home with her from that day's sales. He had earlier visited the barn where the sale had been held and had noticed the cash box at that time. It was almost as if Fate herself had a hand in the affair for there sat the tin box, unattended, on the coffee table in front of the couch and the distinctive sound of Mabel's Jeep driving away. She must have forgotten something and then had forgotten the cash box!

"Yoiks!" muttered Darren as he scurried down from the roof using the TV antennae as a makeshift ladder. The rest of the three person roofing crew were on the other side of the house and wouldn't notice if he slipped into the house and quickly snatched a few twenty dollar bills! Thus he was quite startled to hear the words, "Whatever do you think you are doing?" and he whirled around shocked. What was Mabel doing here? He had heard her drive away!

What Darren didn't know was that that Mabel had an arrangement with a friend to first drop Mable off at her house and to then borrow Mabel's Jeep. Darren dropped the cash box as he whirled which in turn frightened Mable into taking a backward step which bumped her arm against a counter which caused her to plunge the rather sharp knife she was holding with one hand... which had been intended to slice herself the pear she held with the other... upward, into her chest.

"The knife, not the pear," smiled Petra.
Duke laughed.

Darren was a thief it is true, but he had not intended murder and seeing that Mabel was in fact, stabbed as it were, rushed forward with very good intentions, but then he tripped on the edge of the living room area carpet and fell on top of Mabel, propelling the knife deeper into her chest.

"Ugh!" Mabel grunted with the combined weight of Darren and the shock of the deeply driven blade but even that was not enough for poor Mabel for as it turned out, Jeremy Pincher, the town drunk, who lived straight across the street from Mabel had overshot his own driveway, hit reverse instead of forward and backed into the moaning Mabel's front porch with a huge crash, jarring the house and driving the blade even deeper into Mabel's chest.

"Oh no!" laughed Duke.

"Oh my god!" Darren whimpered, rolling off of Mabel who touched the knife as gently as if she were considering its silverware pattern. She then fainted which left a moral dilemma for Darren now didn't it?

Duke nodded in agreement.

But again, Darren was a thief, not a murderer and so, snatching up the tin box, he ran out onto the deck screaming for help. "She's dead!" he howled, "she's dead!" he screeched as he shook the tin cash box,

"and I didn't do it!"

"He did SORT of do it," mentioned Duke.

"That is true," Petra replied.

As it turned out, the rest of the roofing crew had a very good view of the huge wave as it approached from the distance.

"Trade will soon be at a premium in the town of Temagazombie!" said the one and the other two roofers nodded and then, eyes widened in response to Darren's screams, further talks of future business opportunities came to a necessary halt.

Back at the ruined wedding, there were many wet heroes and heroins to be found as they bravely plucked drenched cats and not a few unwise dogs from the torrential river. Tanya the coat check girl made a name for herself that day, boldly swimming across the current to snag what she thought was a small child caught in the branches of a tree. It turned out to be a doll but that didn't make Tanya any less brave, now did it?

"Nope," agreed Duke. "She was brave!"

"Perhaps the true hero that day, continued Petra...

...was Patricia who kept her calm and shepherded as many people as she could into the safety of Lester's house, retrieving her daughter's intended, Rebecca, who stood on a picnic table as if she were Cassandra in her drenched, beaded gown, proclaiming doom for one and all.

"Who is Cassandra?" asked a bewildered Duke, "I don't remember a Cassandra."

"Never mind, Duke," smiled Petra. "It doesn't matter who Cassandra was."

"Okay," Duke smiled brightly.

"So anyway, Patricia, Lester's first wife said...

"Its time to come down now, sweetheart," to her sodden and dramatically hysterical future daughter in law, "everything is going to be just fine."

"Fine?" Rebecca all but screeched, plucking at her ruined gown, "This is a disaster!" Which was true, technically, as in a flood is a disaster but since Rebecca seemed far more concerned with her dress, Patricia sensed that it was not the flood Rebecca was referring to and changed her tact in a flash.

"Rebecca..." Patricia all but crooned, "Come inside, I have a gorgeous after party dress in my bag that will look lovely on you."

Rebecca turned maddened, mascara streaked eyes toward her future mother in law, "What color is it?" she demanded.

"It is the loveliest shade of blue," coaxed Patricia, "It will set off your eyes brilliantly, now do come on down from the picnic table, dear."

Meanwhile, across town, the roofers did what they could to keep Mabel comfortable as they tried in vain to get through to 911. In the end, they carefully lifted Mabel onto a ladder and used it as a gurney and then loaded Mabel into the van. The helpful roofers then rushed her to the hospital after it became clear that the phone line had been busy for far too long.

"That number has been busy for far too long," said the one and, "It's the flood, it must be," said the other while the third gently tucked another drop sheet over Mabel who had regained consciousness while being lifted. Darren still held the tin box as he watched anxiously.

Nobody ever mentioned the discrepancy of certain sixty dollars gone missing to a recuperating Mabel, for really, who knew what had happened to it? What with the flood and as Ernest Tophandle put it, "wet lesbian everywhere!" and how the wedding plans had to be changed to accommodate drenched guests and Mabel being stabbed and Jeremy Pincher getting arrested for drunk parking, in the end, nobody really cared all that much.

...As for Veronica, she was never seen again," concluded Petra sardonically giving Duke a look, *"the end!"*

Lilly could be heard singing, "I am woman, hear me roar..." from inside the ladies room closet.

Mr. Abraham chose that moment to walk into the club. He paused, raised an eyebrow and then walked into his office carrying his new three dimensional puzzle of "The Leaning Tower of Pisa," closing the door behind him with a lift of his chin.

Duke smiled angelically, sighed and then fell into a deep, deep sleep.

IZZY

Izzy was a fashion conscience pixy. She sparkled her way through fashion trends, and her leaf lined closet was filled with a diverse assortment of clothes she had accumulated over the years. She and her friends, Petunia and Meadowlark traded clothes and shoes and hung out at the Four Cobwebs Mall, giggling and twinkling and sometimes sniggering at fairies who lacked basic fashion sense.

"Oh my gizzard," Petunia mouthed, pointing with her head as an oddly dressed banshee walked past the three girls as they found a table and sipped their nectar fizz. "She looks like a troll."

"Petunia, that's not very nice, and anyway, she *is* a troll!" Izzy reprimanded, although her rosebud shaped mouth twitched into a grin. "Don't you remember when we used to be goths?"

"Well sure," said Petunia, covering a delicate belch with one translucent wing. "But we did it with style."

And it was true, Izzy and her friends did have style and were the envy of many of the other fairy teens that hung out at the mall.

Izzy was buxom and blond. Her long legs currently encased in a pair of second hand Sluggs, she wore a cunningly ripped army jacket over a fuchsia colored tank top that sported the words, "Hex My Day." She had teemed it with a ruffled tutu and felt quite pleased with the assemble. It always paid to mix things up a little, she thought to herself, especially if you did not have much to spend. She tore another strategic hole in her ragged pink fishnet stockings and watched a pimply faced dryad stare at her as he walked into a food kiosk. He knocked it over in his distraction, sending steam shooting into the air as the kiosk disconnected from its heating pipe.

Meadowlark, a petite and deliciously droopy water nixie, eyed Izzy's wardrobe choice with envy and once again, wrung water out of her hair as her two friends pretended not to notice. "So, Iz? What style would you call that?"

"What?" Izzy replied.

"That, what you are wearing. The thing with the boots and the other thing."

Petunia hid a smile; Meadowlark was not the most brilliant conversationalist.

"Oh, this?" Izzy smiled at her friend and shared a tolerant and amused grin with Petunia. "I am not sure. Mm. Ballet grunge?"

The three girls tittered and Meadowlark dripped a little as she did. Again, her two friends pretended not to notice. They had been best fae's since glittergarden.

Petunia struck a dramatic pose, she was a selkie and quite proud of her golden tasseled tail. It was the ultimate accessory and simply went with everything, which was just as well as it was attached to her body. "So? What do you think?"

Izzy and Meadowlark eyed their friend and then each other. They had both been dreading this moment.

"Well, it is certainly a bold choice." Izzy murmured diplomatically.

"I like the way you did that with the, um, whatever

and made that dress, uh. Green? Or Blue or. I dunno. Black? Striped and confusing, sort of?"

Petunia boasted. "I bought a glamour for it; you can't tell what colors the dress is. It keeps changing."

It was true, the striped dress continuously changed colors, and while that sounded good in theory, it was rather distracting in practice. Petunia had paired the atrocity with a straw garden hat and painted her goat-ish heels an almost vicious shade of purple. Altogether, it was an alarming outfit.

Petunia's ears twitched eagerly. "I call this look, Shabby Shriek."

Izzy opened her mouth while kicking Meadowlark under the table. "I would never have thought of it," she said honestly. "It is quite the combination. I give you points for originality." She looked up and watched the noon ferry blimp pass over the curved glass ceiling of the food court. "Lunchtime." She changed the subject. "I am going to grab some French flies."

Meadowlark drooped fetchingly, her attire, a dress made out of carefully stitched leaves paired with flu-orescent orange army boots, at first glance seemed at odds with her tiny frame. But she had a knack for combinations and was the recipient of many admiring glances.

"I think I am just going to stick with bogyurt," Meadowlark said.

"Why?" Petunia asked bluntly. "You are skinny as a kelpie as it is."

"Well, you know ..." Meadowlark replied vaguely.

"Petunia is right." Izzy firmly agreed. "Enough with the dieting, real fae like curves."

There came a honking sound and then a whooshing from above as the dirigible discharged its passengers and then honked again as a summons to board.

Izzy looked up, as did Petunia and Meadowlark, people watching being their favorite sport next to fashion and it was Izzy who spotted him first. Her jaw dropped.

"Is that … is that who I think it is?" she stammered.

"Bleg a bug a bip uh …" Meadowlark answered in gibberish while Petunia simply stared.

Striding down the stairs that led to the blimp platform came an all too recognizable young man, attended by a retinue of extremely well dressed, fawning sycophants.

"Oh, my goddess!" Petunia squealed, and she was not the only one. From every direction swarmed a myriad of dryads, pixies, nixies and assorted other fae, armed with anything that could carry an autograph. Some even offering various body parts to be signed.

"It. Him. He." Meadowlark gasped while Izzy stared. It *was* him. The one and only him. That most glamorous of glamorous actors, whose recurring role in the series, 50 Glades of Twilight had girls and not a few boys glued to their seats and squirming.

Brad Spit.

Meadowlark leaped from her chair, knocking it over in excitement and Petunia quickly looked into her ornate compact before joining her friend as they rushed to join the throng of excited fans.

"Brad! Could you sign my wing?"

"Brad, I love you!"

"Brad, I am your biggest fan."

Izzy sat, listening to the shrieks and squeals but didn't leave her seat. She chewed on her lip instead and felt her cheeks redden as she took in the site of the actor. He posed for photographs and signed autographs and just by his very presence, lent an air of magic to the food court. He was clad in a checkered waistcoat with a single top button that allowed his ornate, embroidered silk vest to be displayed. Brad, The Spit himself, whose golden hair was topped by a resplendent pork- pie hat, all trendily squashed looking and sporting a jaunty peacock feather.

Izzy bit her lip again, hand covering a hole in her fishnet stocking, suddenly plagued by feelings of inadequacy.

Brad Spit moved through his adoring fans, waving a gloved hand, his carved wooden walking stick tucked under his other arm. Izzy watched as Brad reached up to pat the cheek of a fluttering fairy, whose wings flapped frantically. His stretched arm raised his coat to reveal striped trousers.

Izzy sighed, earlier pride in her outfit forgotten.

She mooched her bottom lip, frowning and pouting, thinking furiously. What did she have in her closet to come anywhere close to being able to pull off such a dashing look? Nothing. Nothing was what she had. And even if she were to go shopping, she knew that somehow, for all her inventiveness and originality, she was what she was, a pixie, and a rather poor one at that.

Brad Spit was a steampunk fairy, and no fae was more glamorous than that particular breed.

So lost in her envy was Izzy that she failed to notice as Brad and his retinue continued walking in her general direction, even the screams of the many fans fell unnoticed on her pointed ears. Maybe, she thought to herself, maybe if she added a top hat, a cute little green one to match her eyes and a ruffled cravat at her throat. Maybe if she were to buy a bustled skirt and pair that with say, a ribbed corset? She considered how many pucks she had in her gibbet account and gave a shrug of defeat.

She raised resentful eyes that grew startled as they met those of the tee- sidhe star. His warm, brown eyes seemed to smile even as she felt her face settle into a scowl in response. He reacted with a quirk to his lips that caused his famous dimple to appear in his cheek. She narrowed her eyes, and he gave an imperceptible bow in return.

Oh! He was so damned jaunty!

Izzy glared as the star checked his pocket watch and whispered into an attendant's ear, then walked over to where she sat with her army jacket covered arms on the table, hands clenched into fists. She uncrossed her fishnet stocking covered legs and planted her boots on the floor firmly. She leaned forward, green eyes blazing. Jaunty or not, sidhe star or not, she was Izzy, and she was good enough, steampunk tricked out or not!

"So there!" She half shouted and then looked confused, not having meant to say anything at all.

"My lady?" Brad enquired, a puzzled look on his handsome face. Behind him, the throng held at bay by mall security, Izzy could see Petunia holding up a half-fainting Meadowlark. "Holy Shitake." Petunia mouthed at her. Izzy curled her lip.

"My lady?" Brad repeated. "May I be as bold as to ask where you acquired the jacket you wear with such grace and elegance?"

"Oh sure." Izzy snapped. "Make fun of the peons."

"I assure you," he quickly rejoined, "I had no such intention." His sparkling eyes raked over her from top to bottom, and she felt herself blush despite herself.

"Why do you want to know?" Izzy muttered ungraciously.

Brad's eyebrows quirked upward in surprise at her tone. He doffed his hat politely, "I meant no offense, I often accessorize with army and navy surplus. Forgive me." He gave a small bow and made to turn as Izzy sputtered to his departing waistcoat. "I, wow. Okay. Yeah. I can see that. A fitted army fatigue coat or grey striped pants. That would work."

Brad Spit quickly turned, and Izzy noticed that the sidhe star was in reality, not that much older than she was. "Yes," he said eagerly. "And a small Flare Force cap..."

"...with brass buttons." Izzy finished his sentence.

"The tightly wrapped navy trousers with ..."

"Oh yeah! Those with like, a white ruffled shirt with..."

"…suspenders." They spoke in unison, grinning at each other.

"Indeed." Brad beamed. "And may I add, I do like a nicely fitted boot. So, wherever did you find that jacket?"

Izzy opened her lips and then closed them again, unwilling to admit where she had found it.

The pixie and the steampunk fairy eyed each other in the silence Izzy had created, the crowd forgotten.

On a nearby wall, a large clock ticked loudly. Its cogs turned, and its ornate hands clicked in what seemed to be a long drawn out measure of time.

At last, Izzy stated bluntly, "I bought it at a drift store for five pucks."

"The very thing!" Brad responded. "How clever!"

Izzy narrowed her eyes again. "Do not mock me."

Brad shook his head quickly. "No, you mistake my meaning. I do so enjoy a good drifting."

"You?" Izzy rudely asked. "You enjoy drift shopping?"

"Why certainly," said Brad. "I have acquired my finest treasures in drift stores."

"But why would you need to go to a drift store?" Izzy asked in confusion. "You are rich. You can have anything you want to be made up for you with a twitch of a wingtip."

"It is true," Brad Spit said and smiled so warmly that a watching brownie fainted. "But I enjoy not only the fruits of the labor that come with the search but the acquisition of the original over a copy."

Izzy blushed, but her eyes sparkled.

Brad gave a courtly bow, "Would you be so kind as to join me for high tea?"

"I would love to if you don't have a problem with my two friends coming with me."

Brad extended his gloved hand and Izzy placed her hand in his.

"None at all, it is only proper that you are chaperoned."

Izzy gave a serious nod of agreement. For all that her clothes were inexpensive, her self-value was not cheap.

MARIA SANCHEZ

IN A SMALL VILLAGE IN Mexico …

A man walks with a determined pace. His sandaled feet stir up the dust which each step. He wears a sombrero to shield his face from the afternoon sun. He carries a guitar case in his hand and a cigarillo clenched between his teeth. He arrives at a corner between two posts and places the guitar case on the porch of the village store that faces the street.

A passerby greets him, "Hola, Mariachi!"

His is an old guitar; well weathered with many a song. The man in the sombrero carefully takes it out of its battered case and sets both feet firmly. He begins to play. The smoke from his cigarillo drifts into the air beside him, is briefly seen and then disappears into the sky.

A small wagon pulled by a grey burro approaches and this is not an uncommon thing to be seen. The burro is a fine animal and well known to all. His coat is brushed to its highest sheen and he wears a garland of flowers.

The woman in the wagon smiles a gap-toothed grin and tosses a gathered bunch of herbs at the man, who catches them and nods in greeting. "For remembrance," she calls. He nods again, placing the herbs on the porch and touching his sombrero with respect.

The Mariachi man plays his guitar and at first the melody is halting. He pauses and then stops to tune his instrument, then spits out his cigarillo and begins to play in earnest. From a nearby house, a few doors down, comes the sound of an answering guitar.

"Yi, yi, yi." The Mariachi man sings and a voice from around the corner, joins in harmony.

Several children run down the street and hurriedly sit at a respectful distance.

"Mariachi!" And it is if it were a call a bird would make for there was all of a sudden two more guitars and the sound of a woman singing, joining in as if by magic. There was an art to it however it was done. Together the guitars and the voice join that of the man with the sombrero, the Mariachi man.

He smiles, a tooth glinting and begins to dance as he plays, his feet striking a silent beat against the dusty soil. As if they were a collected wave, the others, the children and others who have gathered, all begin to clap and the Mariachi Man gives a shout.

The music quiets but does not stop. It finds its own pattern and begins to weave around the voice of the man in the sombrero, the Mariachi Man, the teller of the tale.

"There once lived a young girl whose beauty was great."

The Mariachi Man's voice is rich and yet, there is a weariness to it as well.

"She was loved by her family and the town that she lived in loved her greatly. She was both merry and generous. Her lips were as red as ripened cherries and her eyes were the deep, rich brown of coffee."

The music seems to sigh and there are other sighs as well.

"Yi, yi, yi!" She was the music when we danced."

The guitars play louder and the woman sings a note that hangs in the air and then echoes into the distance.

The Mariachi stills his dancing feet and begins to speak. The music becomes muted and waiting.

"Maria Sanchez and no, that was not her real name, had many suitors," he says to his audience. "To none of them, would she give her heart. She could not. She had given her heart to her childhood sweetheart, Alendro. Together, the two young sweethearts spent their days beneath the bright sun of a small town with red stucco walls. They laughed and chased the lizards and by night, they listened to the sound of the cicadas."

From the crowd who listens, there comes the clicking sound of the timbales and someone laughs.

"One day, Alendro's father got a job in a bank in the city. Alendro and his family left the little town behind them but not before Alendro offered Maria's heart back to her."

The Mariachi Man strikes a brash chord and the other guitars counter it.

"No," Maria refused. "Know that you carry my heart forever."

The Mariachi Man holds up a hand and the music stops at his command.

"She only saw Alendro once more."

He begins to play again and the music follows him.

"Maria was a lively girl, and she had a smile for everyone. She danced at Festival but never once did she give the smile she had for Alendro to any other man. She danced, yes. Her eyes were merry, it was true. But the other young men were not Alendro."

The music changes and becomes somber.

"One day, Maria felt both tired and sick and took to her bed. Her papa summoned the town doctor to the hacienda and he listened to Maria's heart. "Senor," the doctor said in a most serious manner, "Maria's heart has been broken and it is failing. This is why she has grown so weak.""

A woman sighs and then another.

"Maria's Madre wailed but her papa demanded, "What is this foolishness? We cannot lose our Maria because of a broken heart!""

The Mariachi places a hand on his heart and then resumes his tale, his fingers plucking a sad melody on his guitar.

"Now, Maria Sanchez came from a wealthy family and no amount of *dinars* was spared in search for a cure to her illness," he said. "The town doctor was sent away and Maria was taken to the finest hospital in all of Mexico. The doctors looked at her blood and they looked at her teeth and they listened to her heart but Maria became more and more ill. Her strength weakened daily. In time it was discovered that Maria had cancer and that it had become *Agudo,* which means *Acute* - and means what it does in any language. Maria was dying."

There comes a wailing from the crowd.

"There was much weeping in the town and Maria's Madre sent for her sisters, and her brothers, and her aunts and her uncles and they made food and they prayed. Maria's papa desperately sent for more doctors who came and they went, each in turn holding the young girl's hand and listening to her failing heart. But they all shook their heads in sorrow, for there was nothing more to be done. At last came the day when Maria nodded to herself and asked her Madre to ask the town Mayor to visit her on her deathbed."

The Mariachi man looks around him and nods as yet more people join the listeners.

"The Mayor, was a short man with a balding head and a stern face. He would not have considered himself to be a romantic but Maria's beauty, even as she lay dying, was so great, he could not help his eyes from filling with tears that such a lovely girl was soon to pass from the world.

"Senorita, what may I do to ease your heart?" The Mayor asked, not knowing that her heart was held by Alendro. Maria said to the Mayor,

"I will soon be one who is visited on *Dia de Muertos, The Day of the Dead*. It will soon be to me that people will leave presents. But there is a thing that I would ask to be given to me while I am still alive."

"Anything. Yes." The Mayor agreed quickly, for not only was Maria a girl of surpassing beauty, her family was wealthy and as such, many things were possible."

The music stops suddenly.

"I wish for a man to be brought to me. His name is Alendro Brigado."

The Mariachi Man plays a loud discordant flourish and there comes another wailing sound that is taken up by another. The music swells loudly then gentles and the Mariachi man takes up the tale once again.

"Anything, anything," said the Mayor as he held Maria's pale white hand.

"The problem is, I do not know where he lives. He moved away when I was very young," Maria said and she coughed a delicate cough.

"We will find him." The Mayor promised her, wringing his hands while in the direction of the kitchen the weeping sound of the gathered women rose and fell like the sound of the sea.

"But" Maria added ..." And here, the Mariachi stopped playing and held up a finger, "I want him brought to me by *The Helos Roderos*. Nothing else will please me."

"This was something altogether different," said the Mariachi man and many of the listeners nod gravely. "The Helos Roderos or, in English, The Hell Riders, were a motorcycle gang and greatly feared. This was certainly not a group of which one could ask a simple request, deathbed or not!"

"The Mayor tried to explain this but Maria said,

"This is the only thing that will please me. Ask that the leader of this gang come to my bedside and I myself shall ask him to do this thing, but be quick, death waits for no one."

The Mariachi man grins.

"The Mayor would have pulled at his hair if he had any!"

There is a laugh from the crowd and another joins it.

"But the Mayor agreed to have a message sent to what was the most feared motorcycle gang in the area. *The Helos Roderos!*"

"Iy iy iy!" The singing starts up again and the guitars play a lively tune until it is time once again for the Mariachi man to speak.

"Much to the mayor's surprise, not only did the leader of *The Helos Roderos* agree to come to see Maria, but on the day that he came, he brought the entire gang. Their motorcycles could be heard approaching the town from many miles away, their engines sounding like the thunder before a storm.

The Townsfolk watched in dismay as the gang roared through the quiet town on their motorcycles, weaving between the store fronts and eventually setting up residence nearby in a camp of their own making. *The Roderos* took food and drink as they chose while the leader, a man known only as *Tribule* - which means *Trouble*, visited the dying Maria."

There comes a hiss from the audience, quickly hushed.

"Tribule, for all his reputation, was a kind man and had daughters of his own. He spent the day speaking with Maria, playing cards and making pleasant and light conversation.

Finally, Tribule cleared his throat and asked, "I understand that you wish a man to be found."

"Yes." Maria said. "I knew him as a child."

"You wish to see him, now?" Tribule asked her. "May I ask why?" He gently stroked Maria's pale brow and said, "Bambino, would it not be best for him to remember you as you were and not as you are now?"

"No," Maria told Tribule. "I wish to look upon his face one last time and my greatest wish is that you bring him to me, you and your gang."

"But," Tribule said to her gently. "By sending us, he will be struck with fear, is this at the heart of it?"

"Yes." Maria said. "It is, actually. I gave him my heart and he broke it."

The guitars play on and the sound of a horn joins in mournfully.

"Tribule looked at Maria for a small time and she looked back at him quietly and then, Tribule nodded his head. He would do this thing.

And so *The Helos Roderos* set out to find Alendro Brigada and find him they did. He did not protest when he was led to where the motorcycles stood like impatient horses. Instead, he climbed calmly onto the back of a waiting steed.

Tribule and *The Helos Roderos* roared back into the town where Maria waited on her deathbed listening for their return. Tribule himself led the young Alendro to Maria, her beauty shining as if it were a star."

There is many a sigh from the listening crowd. The Mariachi man sighs as well.

"Maria." Alendro murmured from where he stood at the doorway of her bedroom. "It has been many years."

"It has been," Maria agreed.

"I wish...." Alendro said. "I wish that our meeting could have been under different circumstances."

"As do I," Maria said sadly. "It has been many years since I have heard your voice or seen your face."

"I was young and life happened to me," Alendro said."

From within the small crowd of people who have gathered to listen, a woman hisses and spits and then another and another as well.

"You forgot me," said Maria.

"Never," said Alendro. He fell to his knees beside Maria's bed. "I would give your heart back to you, if you would take it."

The Mariachi man speaks. "A single tear …"

The music stops for one moment and then comes a single note and the Mariachi man says,

"One single tear slid down Maria's face and she wept."

"You would give my heart back to me, broken as you have left it? You would not keep it and make it whole once again?"

"We were children," Alendro said and tears formed in his own eyes.

"Children yes, but you made a promise to me, a pledge. Will you not keep it? You would break this pledge as you did my heart?"

A voice wailed in the distance once more, a voice of a woman, and somehow the voice of many.

"Alendro took Maria's small hand into his own and touched his chest. "I meant the words, but Maria, I was a child when I spoke them. I am now a man."

Maria pulled her hand from his and turned her head away from him, weeping bitterly. "A man? A man who would not honor the pledge that he made! A man who holds my broken heart but would give it back now that it is too late to give it to another to mend? What kind of man is that?"

The women begin to murmur and the Mariachi Man raises his voice.

"A good man," Alendro insisted. "A good man! The boy loves you still, but as a child does."

"No," Maria wept. "You are not a good man or you would honor the vow that you made."

"But I was a child!" Alendro protested, "A child who did not know the words that he spoke!"

The Mariachi man continues.

"The tears on Maria's face did not make her any less beautiful and after some time, Alendro sighed for he could feel the pain in the heart that he held. "It must be then, since you will not take it back from me. I cannot look on your face and see you embrace death with the broken heart that I hold."

The next day, a great wedding was made and the entire town was in attendance, although the Mayor had to send to another town for more food as *The Helos Roderos* had taken much of it for themselves. And it was the leader Tribule himself who gave the bride away."

There were many a raised eyebrow at this but no one spoke.

"Maria held tightly to Tribule's arm as she walked toward Alendro who stood waiting for his bride, her heart in his hands."

From within the crowd of listeners, a woman smiles and her husband holds her close to his chest.

"On the night of the wedding, after the feast, the bride and groom retired to their bed and consummated their marriage."

There is a cheer and some laughter as well.

"And it seemed for a time that Maria would become better. She was happy and her cheeks bloomed like pink roses. She left her deathbed and her family and the town rejoiced. After some time there was a child born and he was named after his father but nicknamed Hearto for he was both of their hearts combined.

The child grew and was much beloved by all but as cold October approached, Maria began to sicken again until she was once more unable to leave her bed. The town wept, greatly saddened for the beautiful young woman who would leave behind her a half orphaned child."

A woman sighs with a remembered grief.

"Alendro," Maria said quietly. "You must give me my heart."

"No!" Alendro shouted. "I cannot! The vow I made as a child and the vow I kept as man forbids this."

"Alendro!" Maria cried weakly and grasped for his fingers. "You must. If you love me, you must give me back my heart and give your own to another so that Hearto will have a mother at his side!"

"My love, I cannot! A vow once given is a vow that must be kept. You yourself have taught me this. None can replace you." Alendro sobbed into her blanket, "I cannot."

"Cannot? Will not!" Maria said wildly and she

reached for a dagger that she kept at her side. "If you will not do this, then I shall have to do it for you!" And she plunged the dagger into her chest, deeply. "Ahh!" She screamed, "You still have my heart, for it is all of me!" And the knife bit deeply causing Alendro to scream from the pain of it.

A woman cries out as if she too had been wounded.

"Alendro did in time offer a heart to another, a woman named Mariella, so that Hearto had a mother at his side. But it was not his own heart that Alendro gave to Mariella but the heart of his dead wife. Mariella was a good woman, and she did not know it in the beginning that while she may have had Maria's heart, she did not have Alendro's... and in time, she grew bitter as the cold of winter.

A year passed and the town's silos were filled with autumn's wheat. Festivities once more began in preparation for *Dia de Muertos* and Mariella knew that Alendro would visit the grave of the beautiful Maria whose heart she had been given.

"I have raised your child as if he were my own." Mariella said angrily. "I have stood by your side as you wept tears for another. Do not go to her grave."

"I must," Alendro said sadly. ""Hearto must leave gifts for his mother."

"I am his mother!" Mariella shouted. "It is me that you should honor!"

"I do!" Alendro shouted back. "I honor you every day, but this is *The Day of the Dead*, and you are alive"

"Alive without love!"

"I honor you," Alendro insisted.

"Honor," Mariella spat. "You married me but do not love me, how is this honor? Or if it is honor, it is honor for your first wife that she asked this of you!"

Many a head nod in agreement at this.

"Alendro could not deny the truth of these words but still, he dressed in silence and took his small son and visited his dead first wife and left gifts on her grave.

Mariella did leave presents for Maria but always did so after Alendro was gone. Year after year she would sit by Maria's tombstone and weep bitter tears. One day as she did, she felt a touch on her cheek .She looked around fearfully and there before her stood none other than Maria herself!"

There is a gasp and a young child turns his face and hides it in his mother's shawl. The Mariachi man smiles with reassurance and plays sweet sounding chords on his guitar.

"Now, Mariella was much afraid but the ghost said to her,

"Mariella. I thank you and bless you for what you have done. You have raised my son as if he were your own and he is now a fine man. I did not wish a lifetime of unhappiness for you in exchange for such a gift."

"He loves you still," Mariella cried. "Take back your heart, for it was never mine."

The music swells with anguish and then quiets as if it waiting.

"Maria took the weeping Mariella into her arms,

and whispered," I will do this thing. I thank you for all you have done. Forgive me."

"I am a good woman," Mariella whispered. "Take back what is yours. I would love another with the years I have left to me."

"Shh," said the ghost of Maria Sanchez. "You will have all of this and more, in return for all that you have done for me."

There is the barest whisper of a melody…

"In time, Hearto made a great marriage for himself and soon had a son of his own. It was another cold, late October and as Hearto left gifts at Maria's grave he also left presents at the grave of his father."

There is another gasp and someone shouts in surprise.

"For Alendro had died unexpectedly in his sleep many years past, his own heart crushed within his chest as we crush the chili."

There came a discordant clash from the weathered guitar and many a gasp was heard from the listening crowd.

It had come as quite a shock to everyone except for Mariella! She was now a wealthy woman and had made a marriage of the heart with another and she smiled every day."

The Mariachi smiles sadly at the listening group of people and then looks down at his hands that have brought the story from the battered guitar. He hums for a few minutes and then reaches to pick up the rosemary the old woman had thrown to him. He holds it to his cheek, inhaling and then speaks at last.

"At his parent's grave, Hearto held his young son close and said, "My child, be wise with who you trust your heart that they do not keep it as their own."

The listeners of the tale nod in agreement and watch silently as the Mariachi, having finished his tale, places his guitar in its case and strides away along the dusty street.

THE CAST IRON SKILLET

AMANDA SLID DOWN THE SMOOTH surface of the washing machine; her back pressed against it; crouched in the darkness and anonymity of the laundry room, hiding. Her husband was too drunk to think of looking for her there, and she almost smiled but grimaced instead. Whoever would have thought she would have ended up in a bivouac beside her Maytag?

She could hear her husband stumbling in the hall, crash, and a curse muttered as he walked into a wall. Again, she almost smiled. For, yes, it had come to the point where she found his drunken state almost humorous. Therein lay the horror, that she could somehow find any of this to be funny.

"You don't pay the bills!" he had screamed, face reddened with rage. What had started the argument, Amanda could not remember, only that it had escalated, and somehow, she was to blame. There was no way around it now; there was nothing she could say that would be the *right* thing, no magic phrase that could placate her husband. The thing would have to run its course, whatever the cause of this fight was not relevant, staying out of his way, was.

Amanda ran the tips of her fingers across the smooth white door of the washing machine almost absently. It was somehow comforting. She patted the machine as if it were a dog and then stiffened as it made a slight sound, its metal frame slightly buckling in response to her ministrations. She listened carefully, her face still and blank. Perhaps her husband had gone outside. Maybe he had gone down to the boat. Maybe she could sneak out of the laundry room, to where she wasn't sure, but her knees were becoming cramped from crouching for so long.

The slightly opened laundry room door allowed her to see into the kitchen. Amanda had a view of the pine kitchen island and its pans and pots and hanging lids, those that were left, for he had kicked the island when he called her a "bitch." The island looked intact, thank goodness; it was a present from her mother, as so many of her belongings were. She didn't know what she would say if it were to become broken, rather, she did, she would have to lie.

Rhyming Simons—a childhood memory of running off the edge of the dock, straight into the water as fast as she is able. Where the name had come from, she never could find out, but she had borrowed the term to mean something more than running into the water. To her, it meant running into danger, and she had been thinking to herself, "It's Rhyming Simons time. My god, its Rhyming Simons time," for the better part of three hours now.

Running to - running from. She had run *into* danger, and now, she was enacting 'hiding *from* danger.' on the days that she cursed herself for being a coward, she remembered this one thing, she was doing Rhyming Simons — yes, but she was also saving her own life.

Amanda flexed, and the washing machine flexed with her, making a slight sound as it did, almost as if it were perhaps agreeing that, yes, she was right, saving her own life was important.

Amanda stared shock-eyed at the kitchen island, askew where he had left it. It was, in actuality, a medium sized cart, with shelves and on wheels, but very sturdy. It solved the need for counter space quite neatly. Amanda blinked.

She could see one of the wooden spoons and the strainer pot where they had fallen, as she listened for the sound of breathing other than her own. She licked her dry lips. He had made her beg.

"Until I think that you are sincere and when I know that you are really, *really* sorry and that you mean it, don't even think to say you are! Don't you dare! And don't you fucking have a cup of *my* coffee in the morning and have fun with the 'nic cravings!" He had roared, "Don't be smoking any of *my* cigarettes, and don't you dare eat any of *my* food!"

He had gone on and on until she had said that yes, she was sorry, yes, she did mean it, and dammit she *was* sincere. The entire time shaking, and yet, thinking to herself as she begged for forgiveness, "Is he really doing this?"

But of course, he really, really was, and it wasn't the first time. However she may have tried to explain it to herself, she didn't understand how her husband, who could be so nice at times could turn into what? A monster? Yes, a monster, and so quickly after he had a few drinks in him.

It was truly astounding how much he could drink. While it was mostly beer that was his preferred beverage, tonight, he had added whiskey. She knew what that meant. She would have to be especially careful, and even that would probably not be enough.

"I have stress!" he had screamed with spittle across her face as she tried not to cringe, tried not to show fear because to show weakness would have made things worse for her. "Stress!"

Well, yes. He did have stress. Everyone had stress, but best not to think about that because she could hear the front door slam as the monster reentered the house from where it had gone. It. He.

He had never drunk so much whiskey; the bottle lay on the floor where he had thrown it, and it was almost empty.

She crouched in the darkness, trembling and willing her cramped legs just to shut up already, enough with the complaints, this was her life, not only her knees that were at stake here.

In Amanda's brighter moments, she thought, "He has never hit me, not really. Pushed, yes. Threatened, yes. Broke things, expensive things. Maybe he will stop, the sun is shining, and he is smiling, and maybe he will see what he is doing, maybe he will."

But in Amanda's darker moments, when the sun was gone when her husband was not her husband but the monster instead, she thought only of getting out. Getting away, escaping if she could, somehow, somewhere. Yes, she sometimes thought about how nice it would be, how convenient, if the monster would just die. A heart attack maybe, or a stroke; either would do just fine. Then he would be gone for good. Yes, she would probably feel bad about it, and she would grieve, but truly, it would be best.

"Where the fuck are you, Amanda?"

She heard him calling from the bedroom. Yes, that was the sound of a crash, and it was probably something expensive too. Her lips curled up into an almost smile again, *why couldn't he break cheap things?* They had so many extra cups. The ones with the turkeys on them were not something she would miss, but it was almost as if the more expensive the object, the more satisfying it was for him to break it. It didn't make sense since so much of what the monster complained about was how badly in debt they were.

"His debt," a voice seemed to say, and it was the voice Amanda called her inner goddess voice. It was a voice of reason, or rather, a voice that tried to reason with her, even if it was only inside where no one could hear it except for her. "His debt," the voice insisted, and this was mostly true.

Her husband did have a tendency to buy things he could not afford. When she asked for something for herself, out of the money she made, the money he took, the money that he kept, her money, on the bank card that was in his wallet and not hers, it became her fault somehow that they didn't have the money for it.

"Amanda!" the monster roared, and she closed her eyes.

"You do not have to live this way," the voice reasoned. "He is in the bedroom, run for the door, and get to a neighbor. Call the police."

"But," she objected. "He is so fast!" And it was true. He could be very fast, and if the police didn't keep him if she couldn't find somewhere far enough away, she knew that this call for help could also cost her dearly. In her dark moments, when that sun did not shine, Amanda knew that if she had her husband arrested, he would track her down and kill her like a dog.

A heart attack or a stroke would solve everything.

"Sweetheart," the voice said. "You can hope for him to drop dead all you want, but it's not something you can count on. Go. Go now! Get up and run! You are in trouble, worse than before. Go! Live now, worry about the rest later. This is your life we are talking about here!"

She almost did. The voice was that insistent. She almost uncurled herself from where she crouched with her arms around her knees, but she didn't, and she could hear that voice inside of her give a sigh of exasperation. She could hear the monster in the living room and knew she had lost her window of opportunity. If he found her, he would be angry, and he had drunk a lot of whiskey.

"But," the voice said firmly, that voice, her inner goddess voice. "He is already angry, there is no help for it now. Get out while you still can."

"I can't! He will catch me," Amanda mourned. "It isn't like I can fight him, he is so strong!"

And this was true, yes. Her husband was strong, but the monster was stronger, and the sun was not shining tonight, no, not at all.

She couldn't fight him, and that is when her eyes

turned to the cast iron skillet that had fallen to the floor with a huge clang when he had kicked the center island, wheeled, cart-thing.

She could hit him with it if she had to. She could tell the police that he had come after her and that she was afraid and had hit him with it out of self-defense. It wouldn't even be a lie. Maybe she could hit him enough times that a heart attack or a stroke would seem like a mercy by comparison.

"Well," Amanda's inner goddess argued. "But could you really? Could you really hit him? Let's look at this reasonably. The skillet is heavy, and you are not exactly known for upper body strength."

"Yes!" Amanda argued back. "Yes, I could! I could use both arms. Get a good solid grip on it and bash his face in with it."

"But what if he died?" the goddess inside of Amanda asked gently. "What if you ended up killing him?"

"What if I did?" Amanda shrieked silently.

"Could you live with that?" asked the voice, and it did seem as if the goddess was interested in the answer. So was the washing machine apparently, for it gave another small ding as Amanda shifted.

"The monster would be dead," Amanda whined. "Dead and gone, and then, and then…"

"Perhaps," the goddess mused. "And yes, perhaps you could live with that today, but what about tomorrow? Could you live with that tomorrow? The day after that? Forever?"

"Yes," Amanda answered in a surly tone, even though

she knew that the goddess was right. There would be no living with it tomorrow. His death would haunt her forever. It wasn't in Amanda to be violent, even if she had to be. Along with the word 'bitch,' came his other word for her, which was 'wuss,' and to Amanda, meant 'coward.'

Amanda dug her fingers into her legs; maybe she was a coward. Maybe she was.

"No, you are not!" the voice said. "But you must decide because the monster is coming closer."

And dear lord, it was true. She could hear him coming, and soon he would see her, and then what would she say? What? "I was cleaning the laundry room in the dark?" No, of course, she could not say that!

"Then, it's one or the other honey. The skillet or you make a break for it, because sometimes, whatever you do, it's going to be Rhyming Simons whether you like it or not."

Amanda jumped to her feet and ran for the skillet, grabbing it as the monster spotted her. As he rushed toward her, she threw it for all she was worth at the center island wheeled cart thing, and she hit it too. The skillet made a crashing sound, and the monster bellowed in surprise. Amanda ran as if her life depended on it because didn't it? Yes, yes it did.

"Rhyming Simons! Rhyming Simons!" Amanda screamed as she ran past her husband, out of the door, and down the street, and into the first driveway that she found.

The sun was gone, yes, and maybe it would be gone for a very long time. But maybe, maybe it would not be gone forever, and the voice gently agreed that this was true.

LAURA LEE, THAT'S ME

Laura Lee shivered and cursed, "You stupid idiot," or would have if not for the ten- month old Doberman puppy who pressed against her legs, shivering.

Laura Lee piled stone upon stone, making a crude circle as Brutus looked up into her face. He almost tripped her at times, but it would not do to scold the dog. They were both scared and alone, and it was very, very cold.

The drifting snow made the landscape an alien one. What once had been scenic trees became at the same time a shelter from the storm and a barrier to the view of any who might be searching by helicopter.

If Baron had found his way back to the car. If her boyfriend could remember where he had left her. Them. Brutus and Laura Lee.

"That's me," whispered Laura Lee. "I am she."

The day had started early and with little cheer. Laura Lee and Baron had argued themselves to sleep. The mood had carried itself into the morning with every traded sentence. The words "Did you remember to pack the compass?" had somehow unintentionally become an accusation of incompetence, although, and Laura Lee could not have understood the irony at the time, the reminder was almost prophetic.

She had discovered that Baron had not packed it, so of course, it was a good thing that she reminded him. However, his reaction was a stony face and averted eyes and an unnecessary shoving of the thing into his backpack. Baron's reaction to the argument was to stay silent and to be rough with things as if the thing itself were to blame.

The plan was to take a drive away from their cabin, which was tucked safely along the shores of a civilized lake and anchored by well-built docks. The cabin had a driveway kept clear of snow and ice by an extremely well lit, flashing snow plow. The plan was to leave this warmth and take a walk along a different lake that Baron had found on a map.

"It's really cold, Baron," Laura Lee said as she stroked her dog's soft ears, ears that she had refused to allow to be clipped. Brutus the Doberman with his whip- long tail, a tail that knocked over coffee cups and ashtrays - but it was a lovely tail for all of that.

"Why do we even come here? It's always the same," Baron complained, and of course, that was the heart of it, her not wanting to change her routine - a routine that somehow had become an offense to him. Why this was so, Laura Lee had no idea, but here they were, stuffing backpacks and driving to some unknown lake to do something different.

"It's starting to snow, Baron." Laura Lee brooded as she looked out of the cabin window. "The snow is coming down and," she repeated, "it's really cold."

His answer was to open the cabin's door and whistle for the dog. Or he could have been whistling for her.

She should not have gone. She should have refused. Her instincts had been telling her not to leave the cozy cabin in an approaching storm. Screaming at her. She should have recognized the reluctance of her dog to leave the comfort and familiarity of the cabin, but Baron had snarled, "You never want to try anything new!"

Perhaps he had been right. Perhaps her craving familiarity was boring. And then, somehow, it was as if all the voices of anyone she had ever known, their cruel and taunting voices were telling her that she, Laura Lee, was wrong. That she was stupid. That she wasn't a team player. Perhaps it was those voices that had caused her to raise her chin and say against her better judgment, "I didn't say that we wouldn't go, just that it's cold."

It was as if her hesitation to venture off into the northern wilderness with a young, shorthaired dog and a man who almost forgot to pack the compass was somehow a crime.

"You never want to try anything new, never," Baron spoke the words as if they were a curse. Boots laced and a hand on her backpack, Laura Lee prepared to do something different. Yes, there was some justification in his words. Laura Lee's attention to routine had become somewhat of an issue for them both, and yes, Laura Lee could even admit that she had become somewhat complacent. Still, these things did not change the facts that it was starting to snow even more heavily and that she didn't quite trust Baron to know where they were going.

But she had followed him out of the cabin, her dog trailing reluctantly behind, into a barely heated car with two-wheel drive and a sullen driver who spoke the occasional word to her shivering, nervous dog and none at all to her.

The visibility had been poor, and the car slid along the road that would eventually lead to some lake somewhere, and there they would take a walk. They would do "Something Different." It all sounded so stupid when she thought about it later. There were many things they could have done that were different. They could have skipped breakfast that morning or gone to The Shores, a lovely restaurant, for brunch. They could have played "Boggle" instead of "Risk." They could have done so many other things, but Baron had insisted on the walk on this different lake, and she had agreed, so at the end whose fault was it? Hers, of course.

"Laura Lee, that's me," she muttered in disgust, as she reached into her backpack with one arm while the other hugged her trembling dog. She felt around for the metal box she had packed. It was a metal oval packed with dry matches and other things, one of them, including a safety blanket that looked as if it were made of tin foil. This was now draped across branches behind her, acting as a makeshift windbreak and hopefully shiny enough to attract attention.

At least Baron hadn't contested the insulated coat that she had put on her dog before they left. Laura Lee did not often argue a point but on this, but where her dog was concerned, even Baron knew she would stand firm.

Laura Lee clutched the smooth cylinder. She would have to take her gloves off again to open it. She found herself wondering if this fact shouldn't be conveyed to the company that made it. She would write a strong letter. She really would.

Dear company that makes the metal emergency kits.

If you have to open one, and it's below freezing and you are stranded in the forest with a shivering ten- month old Doberman Pinscher (who still has his ears and tail, thank you), wouldn't it have made sense - no, wouldn't it be LOGICAL - to make it so that you don't have to take your gloves off to open the darn thing? Yours truly, Laura Lee. (That's me.)

Brutus whined uneasily as Laura Lee took her gloves off to open the kit, shaking out the matches. She already had anything that would burn easily placed inside her rough firepit. Tissues, granola bar wrappers, anything that she could find in her pack or her pockets had been put within the circle of the stones. She shivered beneath the large branches that she had dragged over to the pit to shelter it from the wind.

Earlier, Baron had eventually left the slippery main road to venture on to what looked like a snowmobile trail. The snow was falling thickly against the windshield, and the heater was on maximum. After the car had been bouncing along the slippery, uneven track for almost an hour, she had started to weep. Baron had looked at her with disgust and told her to stop sniveling.

They had stopped at a clearing and Baron had left her and Brutus in the car, stomping away with his backpack and his temper. Eventually, Laura Lee staggered out into the cold, pelted by the snow in search of a different lake.

She trudged along behind him, not having to call to Brutus, who kept close to her side, head down against the wind. Baron's mood had lightened, and he commented almost cheerfully, "It 's not too far now, we are almost there."

But "almost there" had become "somewhere" and eventually to "where?" - They couldn't find the lake nor could Baron lead them back to the path. Before it even seemed likely, before it even seemed possible that it could be true, they were lost. It didn't matter how stupid all this had been; what mattered was that they were alone. What mattered was that it was cold. Somehow, (and it was stupid, but it was true) - they were lost in the woods, and the different lake didn't matter at all anymore.

It was past noon, and they were lost in a forest where all the trees looked the same, and the snow fell thickly, having hidden all of their tracks.

"We will just keep looking until we find the car," Baron had shouted to her through the bitter wind that had risen quickly. It was impossible to say if the tears freezing on her cheeks were those of despair or determination, but Laura Lee refused.

"No!" Laura Lee yelled back. "We will stay exactly where we are and wait till someone finds us."

"Are you out of your mind?" Baron had screamed the words at her as if personally insulted. "Nobody knows we are out here!"

"That's not true," she sobbed. She had not mentioned to anyone that they were going on this little trip, that much was true. But part of their routine, part of their so boring routine was to spend the weekend visiting other people or having them over to visit them.

Surely someone would notice that they were missing. Eventually.

"Eventually?" Baron screeched, after hearing Laura Lee's reasoning. "Eventually? Eventually," he thrust his face at her, "eventually we are going to die out here. Keep walking!" Baron stalked away expecting her to follow, but Laurie Lee did not, and neither did her dog. Baron yelled, "Come on!"

"You have no idea where we are going!" Laura Lee called out, and she wasn't accusatory- this was simply a fact. "Do you even know which direction to go? Have you been checking the compass?"

She knew he had not. And maybe that had been her fault as well. She could have said something, but his face had looked so angry. Laura Lee had kept a nervous check on where the sun was in the sky, but she didn't think that this was going to help either one of them locate the car. Maybe she kept checking the sun's position in the sky to make sure the sun was still there.

Baron pointed first in one direction and then the other, telling her where north was and digging out the compass - that compass. She watched in detachment; she couldn't feel her toes, and somehow that didn't matter. What mattered was, her dog was sitting on her feet crouched like the letter "C" in an attempt to keep his paws off the frozen ground. What mattered was-, and here Laura Lee held her ground as if she were set to guard a holy relic from rampaging villagers- what mattered was that she didn't believe that Baron could find his way back to the car. What mattered was that when you are lost, you stay where you are. "We will build a fire. Someone will find us. We have to stay warm." Laura Lee didn't know if Baron was listening to her or not as she watched him stride off in some direction known only to him, leaving her there with her backpack and her dog since she refused to follow. Baron yelled something about bringing help and then he was gone.

Laura Lee struck a match and carefully shielded her small hoard of makeshift kindling, ready to feed the fire with peeled- off bark and small twigs.

A bird flapped sudden wings and Brutus the Doberman (with his ears and tail uncut, thank you) spooked. She soothed him automatically, intent on her task. She had done her best for him, having tied her scarf around his neck and face and wrapping band-aids around his toes. It wasn't enough, but it had to be enough because it was all that she could do.

The fire caught, and she fed it as if it were an infant. Carefully she built the flame, adding larger pieces of wood that she had gathered. Brutus followed her around miserably, making small, sad muttering sounds and getting in her way until she wanted to scream but didn't.

It was also getting darker. "Stay beside the fire, Brutus," Laura Lee ordered uselessly. She opened the small multitool pocket knife that was in her back pocket. She sawed at the larger branches of nearby pine trees, strangling them with her hands and yanking, carrying them to the firepit, making a mat of fronds, then going back and punishing her hands for more.

It could not be called a teepee by any means, but the branches did become a shelter of sorts. Laura Lee and Brutus huddled together beside the fire, and they did not die for the rest of that day.

The night found Laura Lee and her dog shivering from a wind that pushed at the makeshift shelter with a predatory howl. The nearby pines that towered over them bent with the force of it and one in particular, whose branches stretched toward them with curious fingers, asked, "Laura Lee?"

"That's me," answered Laura Lee cautiously.

"Do you want to die? You can, you know. If you want to."

Laura Lee bolted to her feet, shaking off the dream and it was then that she noticed that Brutus had ceased to shiver. It was at that moment and only then that she truly began to realize that, yes, she could, in fact, die here and so could her dog.

"Wake up, boy!" she cried and massaged him vigorously with her cold hands, having taken off her gloves to wrap around his feet, all four of them, as if she had hogtied him as he lay there in her lap. She slapped his muzzle, and he gave a sleepy growl and muttered, "I'm too tired to play."

"Brutus, you wake up right now! There will be no dying tonight."

Laura Lee pulled Brutus closer, hugging him tightly. There were no tears. She bounced him on her lap as if he were a small child. To her, in many ways, he was.

"Brutus!" Laura Lee insisted. "You wake up now!"

"Why did you bring me here?" Brutus asked sleepily.

"Because I was stupid," answered Laura Lee.

And it was true, she had been, but her dog wasn't going to pay for it, not if she could help it.

All through that long night, Laura Lee fed the fire and talked to her dog. She had always known that dogs make great listeners, but what she hadn't known was that they were also great conversationalists. She supposed that freezing had some advantages.

The trees bent toward them as they listened. "Laura Lee ..." Brutus said, with his nose pressed against her ear. "I love you."

Laura Lee gave him a kiss on top of his furry head. "I love you too, Brutus."

"Do you remember the first time you saw me?"

"Of course I do."

Laura Lee had been working at an animal shelter when the call had come through asking for volunteers. She had said yes without knowing what to expect.

She was one of many that had collected together to rescue dogs from a puppy mill, a tame name for something so gruesome and cruel. The stench was unforgiving, and so were the conditions of the dogs that were packed into their small, filthy cages. Laura Lee worked with other volunteers, carefully placing puppies into towel- lined crates. Why that one puppy had caught at her heart was anyone's guess. She certainly hadn't been looking for a dog. But there he was, and he was hers, or she was his, and here they were.

He had looked at her with his deep and wizened

puppy eyes, his small body thin and starved, and she had heard deep inside of herself a pledge that he would love her forever.

"Of course I remember," she said again as she bounced and rubbed her dog, massaging him. "Of course I do."

"Laura Lee?"

"That's me," Laura Lee responded automatically, hugging her dog closely to her body.

"I think we are going to die."

"No, we will not die," Laura Lee reassured him, wrapping her arms and legs around his unresisting body. "There will be no dying!"

But there was. Baron was eventually located, having never reached the car, finding only a cold and lonely death.

Laura Lee was later told that she was a hero for saving herself and her dog. Perhaps she was, and perhaps she wasn't, but later, while she kept to a comforting routine, she also did at times find different things to do and found different things to try.

Years later, the subject of being lost in the woods would frequently come up, since nothing attracts attention as much as a tragedy. Laura Lee always had the same answer. She would hug Brutus the Doberman, whose ears remained gloriously uncut and whose tail knocked over coffee cups, and she would respond, "What can you say really? I did what I had to do."

THE HIGHWAY

THERE WAS ONLY TWO WAYS to look at it, either he left on his own two his feet or in several bloody little pieces.

The day had started off well. The sun had risen normally, breakfast had been consumed, and the dog was in his outdoor pen, happily chewing on the new doghouse. There was nothing out of the ordinary, no raven with a beady eye, perched on a fence post, glaring with prophecy. There were no warning words written backward, written in lipstick on the bathroom mirror. She did not see a black cat, feel a shadow of foreboding, a prickling of sudden gooseflesh or any other indicator that this would not be a good day.

A good day? A good day that the two of them, together for almost seven years, would not argue over something trivial. A day that would not end with his fist through a wall and her paralyzed with fear. That fear that despite his words to the contrary, might punch a hole into her. A hole that unlike the door, could not be repaired with plaster.

There had been some improvements. She doubted she would have stayed if there had not been. There had been less drinking for one thing, except for when there was too much of it. There had been the anti-depressants, not for her, although there were many times she had considered asking for them. He had been on the pills for months now, and they did seem to be helping except for the days when they didn't.

There had been the anger management classes, again, not for her but stipulated by her because the last time was to be the last time. The classes did not seem to be accomplishing all that much, the fact that he was going was astounding in itself and surely meant that her threat to leave him had been taken seriously. Didn't it? *Didn't it?*

Couples therapy had been a bust, and the counselor had finally terminated the sessions. Perhaps this should have been her raven, her black cat. But hope is a strong thing, a marvelous thing, except for when it is as blinding as looking into the sun and seeing black spots dancing in front of your eyes. When hope it is not a shining beacon across an expanse of dark waters but the dark water itself, that hope has drowned itself in, weighted down with empty promises.

It started with a phone call, but it could have been anything. It could have been that he had read her text messages and misunderstood a simple dialogue between friends. Why he read the texts was not the issue, or not the only issue, but a broken lamp was the result of it, and it had been a pretty lamp.

"You are planning on leaving me!"

"We were just kidding about how nice it would be to go and live on an island and be served coconut drinks by cabana boys! It was a joke!"

And, crash went that lamp.

"You are lying to me, again. You are lying!"

But there was her house on the one end and her mother on the other.

There was no doubt that her mother loved her, none at all. Long forgiven were the party jokes of how her mother had tried to abort her by sitting in a cold bath after drinking a bottle of Vodka, had deliberately fallen off of a horse, had gone skiing when she had been advised not to go. Her mother had made this up to her in many ways, and if she didn't seem to like her only child, she did love her. She did. Presents and praise almost made up for the almost constant criticism. Therapy, hers, not her mothers, had almost made up for the rest.

"You are gifted and talented; I am so proud of you. But you should have stayed in school. You should never have gotten married, had children. Look how that turned out! The marriage is over, and your kids? Don't even get me started! I have always been there to pick you up when you have fallen, and you always fall! I have failed you by helping you. Now come and live with me! It's always me! You leave him before he kills you. You leave him, or I will disown you like I should have done years ago. All you do is take! Don't you see what this is doing to me? I will send you money, a truck and you will live by my rules and be happy."

Her mother meant well. She did. There was never any doubt about that. She had been generous to a fault. But there was also no doubt that if she has never had a child, it would have been vastly preferable.

"I never wanted children!"

And you couldn't say that her mother was a liar either.

And so that day, it was the phone call that started it, and he had been drinking. "I only had two beer!" And this was as possible as it was unlikely as he kept the case in the shed so she really couldn't say for certain.

But his voice had been slurry when he answered the phone. Perhaps he was tired, and that was the reason, or perhaps it was more than two beers that he drank, but that didn't matter either, what mattered was that she was a liar and for what, she was not sure.

His son had blamed her for something when he got into trouble for something by the ex-wife who had said something. This was all that she knew as she was trapped against a closed door, and that fist was pounding through that door as he screamed at her.

And what could you do? What you did not do was move. What you did not do was make eye contact. What you did not do was say anything, not a word. You froze, and you waited for the right time to say you were sorry because that was all you could do except make a run for it, and he was fast as a hungry snake with a rat in its sight.

She had waited and placated, and when he had stormed off, she had phoned the police as she said that she would do if this were to happen again. This was the last time she had said, although not out loud. This was what she could do, and so she did it, and if it were to be her mother's money and her mother's truck, even though her mother didn't like her, she loved her, (she did). And if it were to be her mother's house and her mother's rules then so be it.

The police came as she hid in the tenant's apartment, listening to the angry footfalls from upstairs as he looked for her, cringing as the tenant's phone rang as he sought for her there.

The police took him away, but they did not arrest him, for reasons she did not understand. She knew she only had so much time and so, it was boxes and packing and closing bank accounts and not running as she knew that she should, taking only as much as she could carry and a leash on her dog.

And she had almost got away with it, the truck booked and her mother waiting and the house calling to her, but he had come back.

And he had been sorry.

"Don't listen to him!" Her mother screamed. "If you do, I will take everything away from you; you will have nothing. I will hate you forever. Is it worth a house on a lake?"

It was indeed a beautiful house, and there was peace to it that had claimed her. A home she had never expected to find and so no, it was not worth the fear, but it was worth something.

And he was sorry. This time it was because he had forgotten his medication and perhaps that was true, that he had run out. Everyone knows you don't just suddenly stop taking anti-depressants like that. Maybe it was true that she shouldn't have said whatever she had said that had caused her to be the blame for whatever it was.

Maybe.

"You come here right now! My God, you are so stupid." Her mother shrieked into the phone. "You have always been stupid. My sister has children she can brag about! Look what I have!"

"Stay," said the house on the lake.

He had the filled prescription of anti-depressants, and he had taken one too. He had a bottle of pills to help with his anxiety as well. Somehow this was meant to be his proof to her that he needed them. But she was still to blame for the holes in the closet because she had stood in front of the door and had not moved (could not move). He could not take a walk to cool off with her standing there, now could he? It didn't matter that there was a back door. That was immaterial. She should have moved even though she couldn't move.

He was sorry enough to help her unpack even as he told her she was stupid to have packed in the first place. He was sorry that she had booked a truck to leave, even as he told her she was ridiculous to have considered it. He was sorry that couples had fights, even though she still wasn't sure what it had been about. He was sorry that she thought he had been drinking, even though he had only drunk two beers, not enough to make him slurry, no, not at all.

And maybe he was sorry enough to die; she thought to herself as she ground up the pills he had been given for the anxiety that she had caused, grinding them up finely and stirring them into his coffee.

"Maybe," said the house on the lake.

IT ALL ENDS WITH A POEM ...

As it was then
In the hearts of men.
Despair.

For the sea was deep
and the sky too wide.

The houses strong,
consumed by fire.

The rain, it fell
on storm lost ships.

The hearts of men
screamed out in rage
and injured pride.

Through slander
and slaughter
they proclaimed their strength
one to the other.

The snow fell cold
to blanket the dead.

The sickened and spared
lifted trembling fists.

The children, quiet
with arms grown thin,
huddled together
numb with frost.

Once and Again
By Shebat Legion

BIBLIOGRAPHY

Silicon Oar
UnCommon Origins Fighting Monkey Press 2017

Mitten's Pockets
Twisted Tales Volume Two 2018

Lamp-basted

Whatever Lola Wants
UnCommon Origins Fighting Monkey Press 2017
Ladies and Gentlemen of Horror 2017

Father's Day
Slice Girls CHBB Publishing 2015
Ladies and Gentlemen of Horror 2017

Pop, Goes The Zombie
Twisted Tales 2017

The Cookie Lottery
Terror By Gaslight Iron Clad Press 2014

The Apple
UnCommon Origens Fighting Monkey Press 2016
Group Hex Volume One Greater Lake Horror Company 2016
Ladies and Gentlemen of Horror 2017

My Kraken
Klarissa Dreams 2014

Sasha Brook
Darklight Four CHBB Publishing 2014
Ladies and Gentlemen of Horror 2017

Saltwater
Tales of the Fairy CHBB Publishing 2014
Ladies and Gentlemen of Horror 2017

This Island, Barney Templeton

Dree, On Wednesday
Hoblin Goblin Vamptasy Publishing 2012

An Ankh For Becky's Mother

Bartholomew and The Burgler
Klarissa Dreams 2014

A Bird in Hand
Tales of the Fairy CHBB Publishing 2014
Ladies and Gentlemen of Horror

The Day That Many Things Happened
Hot Ink Press 2013

Izzy

Maria Sanchez
Scare Me To Sleep 2016

Ladies and Gentlemen of Horror 2017
The Cast Iron Skillet
Rise of the Goddess CHBB 2014
Group Hex Volume Two Great Lakes Horror Company 2017

Laura Lee, That's Me
Read For Animals 2014

The Highway
Dark Corners Iron Clad Press 2011
Ladies and Gentlemen of Horror 2017

www.ingramcontent.com/pod-product-compliance
Lightning Source LLC
Chambersburg PA
CBHW070502200726
48293CB00007B/2342